SHAWNEE ALLEY FIRE IS HOT!

"HIGHLY RECOMMENDED....This novel...should be a strong Edgar contender for best first novel....Douglas is an excellent writer with a good feel for character, dialog, and most of all setting....Harter is a hardworking, no-nonsense detective. I hope we see more of him."
—*Mystery Scene*

"THOROUGHLY SEDUCTIVE MYSTERY DEBUT.... Quietly enthralling and memorably evocative (with echoes of Hammett's *Red Harvest*), the most auspicious of the many recent mystery debuts."—*Kirkus Reviews*

"A FIRST-CLASS TALENT....Douglas brings the elements of his story together with great skill."—*Booklist*

"A cliffhanger....colorful....builds to a suspenseful climax."—*Muncie Star*

"ORIGINAL....An unusual first novel."—*Newsday*

"A haunting novel...A mystery novel with genuine character, a freshly observed scene, a sense of social history and a distinctive voice."—*Scottsdale Progress*

"As a novel, it's an intriguing 'slice of life'...as a mystery, it's a corker."—*Daily Press* (Newport News, Va.)

SHAWNEE ALLEY FIRE

John Douglas

ST. MARTIN'S PRESS/NEW YORK

SHAWNEE ALLEY FIRE

Coppyright © 1987 by John Douglas

Library of Congress Catalog Card Number: 87-4476

ISBN: 0-312-91003-7   Can. ISBN: 0-312-91004-5

Printed in the United States of America

First St. Martin's Press mass market edition/May 1988

10 9 8 7 6 5 4 3 2 1

For Bob

For men and women are not only themselves, they are also the region in which they were born, the city apartment or the farm in which they learnt to walk, the games they played as children, the old wives' tales they overheard, the food they ate, the schools they attended, the sports they followed, the poets they read, and the God they believed in. It is all these things that have made them what they are and these are things that you can't come to know by hearsay, you can only know them if you have lived them.

—W. Somerset Maugham, *The Razor's Edge*

...

JACK REESE

...

··· 1 ···

I'm only human.

I noticed her nylon-brown legs before I saw her face.

I don't like to admit it, considering everything that's happened since that morning.

But I can plead partly innocent. I didn't notice her legs first simply because I like women's legs, which is no crime, or because she had fine ones, which she did.

You have to picture the scene to get it straight.

The house is built into the mountainside in such a way that the fierce slope of the fire-escape hill in front means you have to walk down five steps from the pavement to the level of the front porch.

I was standing on the porch, sifting through the bills the postman had brought, hoping for that check in the mail, when I heard her heels strike the sidewalk.

I glanced up just in time to see the bend of her knee as she stepped down. Not used to visits from classy ladies, or from ladies at all, for that matter, I wondered what was going on.

I'm not positive I ever got a reasonable answer.

You have to understand, I probably wouldn't have taken her job if I'd known what it involved.

No, that's not exactly right. Words give me trouble. That's why I'm not a writer.

Try again: I probably wouldn't have taken her job if I'd known what it involved—*and* if I hadn't been scrambling to make some sort of a living, waiting every day for that elusive check in the mail.

It was a hard-times fall, that fall of 1982. Not just for me, either. Shawnee, and most of the country, was sunk in a recession. They never called it a depression, though I can't explain the difference to you.

In the midst of it, she sneaked up on me.

Or *snuck* up on me, as Tattoo would say.

She came down the steps from the street and my eyes took her in like a camera panning upward.

High-heeled brown shoes strapped across trim ankles.

Loose tan skirt ending at mid-knee, above those good legs.

Chocolate sweater hiding the fullness of her breasts.

Tan jacket, matching the skirt, adding a businesslike reserve to her outfit.

Red lips, makeup immaculate, green eyes.

Brown hair to her shoulders and sort of flipped under at the ends.

"Are you the photographer, Jack Reese?" she asked in a calm voice I couldn't quite place. She had a certain Shawnee tone but it was overlaid with a studied precision, like she wanted to make it clear she knew her ABCs.

"Yeah," I answered. "What can I do for you?"

"Are you a *good* photographer?" she asked, giving me a wise smile to show she saw the ridiculousness of her question.

"On par with Ansel Adams." I smiled back.

Actually, I've never claimed to be the best camera clicker around. I'm surely not the most successful. Nor am I one of those guys who loads you down with chatter about shutter speeds and exposure times and darkroom expertise. I just do what I have to do to get the image I want on film. Then I do what I have to do to make a decent print of it. At these tasks, I'm more than competent.

"I probably don't need Ansel Adams. I'd just like a passport picture taken," she said.

"Sounds simple enough. Just a head shot?"

"That should do," she replied, her voice turning more like business.

"Come on in and we'll try it."

I opened the screen door and motioned her to enter. I was immediately embarrassed about leading her into the front room. Until I saw her standing in it, I'd forgotten the shape it was in. Not only did it need a new wallpapering, but the room itself was a full-scale mess. I'd furnished it sparely with secondhand odds and ends. Photos, books, magazines, catalogues, newspapers, and old mail were piled all over. A coat of dust was beginning to cover everything.

"I'm still getting set up," I explained.

"Did you just move in?" she asked. "I only today noticed your sign."

A month before, I'd attached the sign, rather like a shyster's shingle, to one of the wooden columns that held up the front porch roof. I'd been careful to hang it high enough so it could be seen from the street.

"I moved here in early August," I told her, deciding to cut short a story I'd been shortening with each retelling. "I used to live in this house when I was a kid and I recently came back to Shawnee." She didn't need to know more about me.

I led her around the staircase that rose up through the middle of the narrow house, bisecting each of the three floors into front and back rooms.

"The studio's a little neater," I said, flipping the light switch. "You can sit on the stool over there."

With careful steps, she crossed the worn rug to the stool. She scooped in the back of her skirt with her right hand and knelt to place her purse nearby. Then she seated herself on the stool, crossing her legs away from the camera and smoothing out her skirt. She moved like a woman used to wearing a dress, not jeans.

As she waited in almost formal silence, I went to work adjusting lights, until there were no shadows on her face or on the screen behind her. I'd done my best to make a simple studio out of what had once been a den and, in later years, a TV room. I'd left the space mostly empty of furniture and covered the windows so natural light didn't confuse the artificial light.

"How long will it take for you to have the photograph ready?" she asked, breaking the silence.

I stopped focusing the camera and looked out from behind the tripod. "How soon would you like it?"

"Tomorrow?" She folded her hands and rested them on her knee. She wore no wedding ring.

"No problem." I wasn't exactly overburdened with work. "I'll take three or four shots and you can pick out the one you want. Passport size, right?"

She nodded.

"Are you going away real soon?" I asked, trying to relax her.

She didn't answer, and I thought I sensed her tense. I guessed she just wanted to get the picture-taking over with. Some people are like that.

Her smile for the camera was different from the rather sly one she'd flashed when she'd asked if I was a good photographer. It was almost as demurely frozen as Mona Lisa's. Behind her eyeshadow and lashes, there was a wariness in her eyes that I'd seen before, that every camera clicker has seen at one time or another. The camera changed her personality. I could tell she didn't feel natural in front of its cocktail-party gaze.

"You really hate getting your picture taken, don't you?" I said after I'd clicked the fourth shot.

"Do you require a deposit or anything?" she asked, stepping off the stool.

"No, just a name."

"I'll be back tomorrow afternoon," she said, bending to pick up her purse.

Then, rapidly, she walked out, making her way without escort through the front room's rubble.

··· 2 ···

Tattoo was coming up through the hilly yard when I went out onto the back porch that evening. A brown bag was swinging from his only hand.

He'd been nicknamed Tattoo by his railroad buddies because he'd come home from the Navy in World War II with a tattoo on his left forearm. It was of a girl in a slinky dress. Her body rippled when his muscle tensed. May had never liked it.

I only remembered the tattoo vaguely. I was still in elementary school when he'd lost the arm that some Tokyo artist had affixed it to.

"May had a craving for some ice cream," Tattoo called to me as he climbed the steps on his side of the porch. "You want some?"

"No. Thanks. I just ate."

"Whatever you say," he said, opening his door and disappearing into the kitchen.

Tattoo and May had lived in the other side of the house since I'd been a kid. They were like uncle and aunt to me.

We often entered through our back doors because cutting through the alley and up the backyard eliminated a block of the steep, rising sidewalk out front. Besides, the old country people usually lived in their kitchens. Tattoo and May, like my grandfather and most of my older relatives, had come to Shawnee from the hills and hollers to work for the railroad years before. They'd brought with them a lot of ancient mountain ways—more than I'd ever been able to fathom.

I guess you'd call the house a "duplex," though I'd never heard the word until I was older, just as I never remember hearing the word *Appalachia* until I sat in a boring sociology class and listened to a flatland college professor play expert about life in the poor-man Appalachians. We ourselves always said we were from East Shawnee, or just Shawnee, or maybe "from the mountains," or—if really pressed—"from the Alleghenies."

I stepped off the porch and walked down through the yard, past the line where my mother had once hung out clothes. She'd always been so careful to bring in the laundry as soon as possible so the grit of the city and the tracks didn't cover it.

At the foot of the yard, by the alley, I leaned against the rusting Ford that had brought me home to Shawnee. The car sat in a space I had cleared and leveled for it. Once a fence had divided the yard from the alley, but it had tumbled down long ago.

The landlord should really rebuild it, I told myself.

Yet I hadn't.

Though it was well before seven, the streetlights in the alley were already fighting the dark. The October days were shortening toward winter.

Looking down the narrow blacktop-and-brick alley, I saw old Daniel sitting on his swing, as he often did. Past my house, the alley they officially called Baxter Street broadened out a trifle, and the lay of the land changed enough to allow a few houses to be built in a triangle between two more major streets. Daniel's was the nearest of the alley houses.

He'd seemed old as long as I could remember—so old I was surprised he was still breathing when I'd returned to the city. I imagine he'd only been in his late fifties when I was a kid playing ball in the alley, but to a kid, late fifties is ancient.

Shortly after I'd come home to Shawnee, I'd spent an August afternoon sitting on his porch swing with him. Daniel, maybe eighty-five, had watched the occasional car go by, momentarily breaking up the games of another generation of kids. That afternoon he'd spilled out one tale after another, some pretty salty. He was not at all the drab old man I'd once thought he was.

Slowly I'd tried to convince him to let me take his picture. He had been reluctant at first because he didn't understand why, but he finally gave in. I'd been happy with the portrait, with the way the lines were strip-mined into his face while the eyes retained a coal-hard purity.

He was a proud man in the way that old working-class mountaineers could be, like my grandfather had been, like Tattoo was. He was also lonely. He had no May, and no relatives came to visit, only a few old railroad pals and, a couple of times a week, the woman who drove a van around Shawnee, delivering hot lunches to the elderly for the Commission on Aging.

He'd told me he hadn't wanted the lunches at first, not liking the idea of someone taking care of him. But then a pretty young girl had come and talked to him and told him how he'd worked and paid taxes all those years, so he might as well enjoy it. Railroad retirement not being exactly the top-of-the-line executive plan, he'd given in.

I looked away from Daniel's porch and turned toward my own house, studying its outline against the darkening sky.

I'd inherited the three-story structure from my grandfather. It was laid out in such a way that if you entered through the back door, you were in the kitchen, which was below street level on the front side. Tattoo's half of the house was a mirror image of mine.

Off the kitchen was the bathroom, installed indoors about the time I was born. Aside the kitchen was a half-basement. Dug right into the mountain rock, it got wet in heavy storms. I'd jerry-built a darkroom in the basement, using the old laundry tubs.

Up the dark staircase and you got to the main floor, where I'd been trying to establish the photography business.

Up the final flight and there were two bedrooms, one on each side of the steps, not a safe arrangement for sleepwalkers.

The house was the reason I'd moved back to Shawnee after fifteen years of living away. The house and the recession.

I'd lost a good chunk of my income in May when the small magazine I'd been working for had folded under the weight of lost advertisers, fewer readers, and postal-rate hikes. While the magazine had never paid me a fortune, it had given me a small base income to operate from as well as the excuse to go places and the time to freelance. Over the years, I'd managed to find a string of publications, mostly tiny and specialized, to sell photos to. Still, without a regular paycheck coming in, it was hard to keep up with big-city costs. I grew to depend more and more on the rent checks from my grandfather's house in Shawnee.

Then, in mid-July, I'd gotten the letter. The guy who'd been renting one side of the house had been laid off from Shawnee Steel with no prospects of being called back. He'd decided to pack up his family and head for the Sunbelt—Florida, Texas or California. He wasn't sure where. He just wanted to get out before his savings disappeared and winter struck.

So he'd played Okie and driven off.

Spurred by the moment, I'd decided to move too. I had nothing to lose. With a place to live for free in the mountains and a few magazine contacts, I figured I'd wait out the depression. Shawnee beckoned.

Since then, I'd eaten a lot of tomato sandwiches, as my

grandfather told me they had in the 1930s Big One. The tomato plants had been left by the former tenant.

I'd tried to be frugal. Ben Franklin would have loved me. About the only luxury I spent money on was film, and that's hardly a luxury to a photographer.

I spent a lot of my days simply roaming Shawnee, clicking my camera at old railroaders like Daniel, at unemployment lines, at derelict buildings, at everything I saw around me. I was determined to document the Shawnee of the 1980s in the same way Walker Evans the Miraculous had once pointed his camera at the stoic faces of dust bowlers and sharecroppers and allowed their black-and-white angularity and their proud, scared eyes to speak for themselves.

Nothing *fancy*, you understand. Nothing too slick.

I clicked roll after roll, at first not sure what I'd ever do with them. They all blended, click after click, frame after frame, in my head, like photos in a Muybridge series.

Eadweard Muybridge is another of my black-and-white heroes, even if he spelled his first name weird.

Story is, he was hired to settle a bet by the governor of California. (Not Ronald Reagan—this was in the 1880s.) Muybridge was asked to prove if there really was a moment in time when all four hooves of a racing horse were off the ground. He clicked one shot after another of a running steed with a contraption he had devised for the occasion, showing how each motion flowed into the next.

Muybridge went on to trap other animals, including people, in action. He did a series of a naked lady kicking a pith helmet, which I like to pretend was his social commentary on Queen Victoria's British Empire. The lady faces us—faces Muybridge's camera—full sex, full pubic hair, long before *Playboy*—and raises high her fleshy thigh, and her breasts bob slightly and the pith helmet flies away from her foot and finally falls to the floor, like Newton's apple. Then she turns away from us—away from the camera—and picks up the helmet and kicks it again to show off the flex of her buttocks.

Take any photo from the series, let it kick on its own, and you can imagine the motions that came before and after.

Any picture could really be the start or the end.

Just actions trapped in time and space by the camera.

Like words, time and space give me trouble.

My problems with words, space, and time only grew more complicated after I moved back to Shawnee.

··· 3 ···

"Ain't it a mangled, screwed-up mess?" declared Tattoo.

I mumbled agreement but kept on peering through the camera hole, trying to line up a good shot of the scrap-metal engine, the twisted track.

"Why bother with the picture?" he asked. "They won't use it anyway."

"Then why did Metling call me out of bed to run out here?"

"They're just going through the motions, Jack."

I looked out from behind the camera. "Tell me what you're trying to say. I like it much better when you're blunt than when you hint around."

While Tattoo could ramble on with the best of the old railroaders, he could also be damn blunt.

He scrunched up his lips and rubbed at the stump of his left arm before he spoke. "I've lived in this city all my life and I know the Shawnee—Potomac don't get no bum publicity in *The News*. Notice they sent you out here, not one of their regular camera wielders. They'll only put your picture in the paper if they can pin this wreck on some poor working slob. Employee error, they call it, like some fellow made a crap wheel on purpose, or some engineer set out to kill hisself. If it turns out this thing was caused by bad tracks, the company'll get touchy and nothing'll be in the goddamn paper."

"Not my decision," I said, clicking my third shot of the flopped over, partly crushed diesel. "I'll get paid whether they use my photos or not. Besides, the engineer didn't die. No one died. Tell the truth. Have you got a grudge against *The News*?"

"I remember too good all those damn editorials they used to write when the union went out on strike. You'd think we was communists. It's the kind of thing stays with you a long time, like a fierce burn. When you think back on it, you get hurt and mad all over again."

"I never wrote any of those editorials. I doubt Metling did either. He's not that old."

"But would he?"

I had no answer. I didn't know what Metling would or wouldn't write, or what *The News* would print if labor troubles arose.

Labor troubles: no such thing, the old union men used to say. There are only capitalist troubles. Fat chance of there being capitalist—or labor—troubles in 1982, when half the U.S. feared joining the unemployment lines even if they were *complacent* employees.

Still, the old men remembered the old times and I should have remembered they remembered. Their anger burned with a low flame that could be turned up at the flick of a hand.

I maneuvered away from Tattoo so I could catch the engine at a different angle. I wanted to show the cab on its side, with the arching loop of ribbon rail pushed out from the ties behind it.

I was glad I hadn't had to decide whether or not to show the bleeding, moaning engineer being removed from the wreckage. Maybe that's why I wasn't a world-renowned photographer. I don't normally go for the blood. I can't stand the television

footage of the wailing masses at Mideast funerals, or the news-
man who pushes a microphone in some griever's face and says,
"What did you think when you saw your husband crushed in the
garbage compactor?"

I'd had no regrets that the state police and railroad bulls had
kept us back from the wreck until there were no accident victims
to see.

The police had said the engineer was the only one seriously
hurt, that the others had walked away under their own power.
The engineer had been ambulanced to Shawnee City Hospital. I
guessed Metling would send a *News* reporter there to learn his
condition, and that someone was already working to uncover
the story of what had caused the derailment in the first place.

I snapped another picture.

"Didn't your Grandfather Reese die in a train wreck?" asked
Tattoo.

I nodded. He knew the story but he was always asking questions like that. Whether he was trying to fill in gaps in his
knowledge or rubbing the scab off memories to make people
remember the wounds, I didn't know.

Actually, Tattoo probably knew more than anyone else about
the histories of Shawnee's railroading families. He'd worked
hard for the union much of his life, though he'd never held a
cushy leadership job. After he'd lost his arm in the accident,
he'd had plenty of time to collect his data.

They'd gotten him back to work as fast as they could.
Shawnee–Potomac policy was that it was better for a man to sit
on the job all day than to sit at home. There was always some
chore even an injured man could do. Maybe sort out a bin of
screws and bolts. By keeping them on the job, the company
could point to signs proclaiming THIS DIVISION HAS LOST ONLY
9 MANPOWER DAYS DUE TO INJURY OR ACCIDENT THIS YEAR.

At first they'd installed Tattoo in one of those shanties by the downtown tracks, where, for eight hours a day, he sat and talked with the older railroad men who dropped in. The only time the conversation stopped was when he had to step outside and hold up traffic to let a train go through the heart of town. Then, in the early 1960s, they'd replaced the signmen with traffic lights and assigned them to odd jobs until they could take early retirement or disability or whatever.

"How did your grandfather die?" probed Tattoo.

"You know it better than I do, I'm sure. It was long before I was born. Not long after World War One. Not exactly the stuff of Casey Jones ballads."

"They didn't write no ballads about most men," he said.

"Well, they tell me he was an engineer. He never got out of the South Shawnee yards that night. Somebody had switched two freights onto the same track. It was a head-on collision. They weren't going fast, but I suppose it was fast enough that the engines were melted together by the heat of the blood."

I walked away from him again.

From straight in front of the long freight, I aimed down the right side, trying to capture the accordian folds of the upset and tilted cars. At the far end of the camera's depth of field, a new Japanese truck was hanging two wheels off the upper deck of an automobile carrier, ready at the slightest tremor to kamikaze into the gravel alongside the tracks.

This was the photo.

I clicked again to cover myself. Then again.

If Metling didn't like it, if Tattoo was right that he'd be careful about what he used, then I'd find another market for it. Since August, I'd sold a few photos to a small rail-lore magazine.

Another possible project had also begun to grow in my mind: *a book.*

Much worse photographers than I had put out photo books

on every inconceivable subject in the last decade. Some of them had so little reason.

So why not a picture book about trains or Shawnee railroaders or 1980s' hard times?

Maybe.

At least it gave me something to pretend I was doing, when what I was really doing was biding time walking the streets clicking a camera and hoping that if I walked long and far enough, I'd get somewhere.

Lifting the camera from around my neck and then slipping the strap over my shoulder, I turned to Tattoo. "You ready to go?"

"I been ready," he said.

We walked through the weeds toward the Ford parked at the edge of the highway.

"Is it ten yet?" I asked. I don't wear a watch myself.

In one of his odd quirks, he raised his right wrist to eye level rather than look down. "Just after."

"Good, I've got plenty of time to get these pictures made." Being a morning paper, *The News* didn't really get serious until after supper.

"Give my best to kindly Mr. Metling when you deliver them," Tattoo said sarcastically as we climbed into the car.

I started the Ford up. After making a U-turn onto the highway, I accelerated toward town, thinking about how visiting the wreck had brought back so many buried things—the oral traditions of head-on tragedy, the anger still inside the old men. I seemed to always be digging up buried elements as I made my way around Shawnee.

I'd only driven a mile or so when suddenly, on impulse, I stopped the car, grabbed the camera from the seat beside me, and climbed out. Tattoo hung his head out the window and watched me.

For some reason, I took a photo of a black-and-white sign:

SHAWNEE

*Shawnee was established in 1754 when
a fort was built to protect settlers from
raids by the Shawnee Indians who hunted
and camped here before the white man.
During the Civil War, Shawnee was
crucial to the Union because of its rail
and canal industries, and because Shawnee
offers the easiest land route through
the mountains to the West.
Long the railroad hub of the Alleghenies,
Shawnee was the second largest city in
the state until 1959.
The Chamber of Commerce
Welcomes You*

··· 4 ···

The Ford was running fine for a seven-year-old car with over 125,000 miles on it. It had had plenty of rest. I'd only driven it a couple times a week since coming back to Shawnee. I had little need for a car, though I knew life would be tougher without one.

I also knew life would be cheaper without one.

When I was a kid, we'd survived without wheels. It was possible to walk anywhere in Shawnee worth going to. We'd walked up the fifty-percent grade to school. We'd walked downtown to stores and movies. We'd hiked through the patches of woods in the unusable gullies between hillsides. If we went far enough through the tunnel of trees, we'd come out the other end into the orchard countryside, where we'd swipe Stark Delicious apples, the ones with the bumpy bottoms.

Shawnee was—is—a small city with less than forty thousand people. Twenty years before, there'd scarcely been any suburbs, though it had sprawled some since, as all towns seem to have. The guts of the city hadn't physically changed so drastically in the years I'd been away, though.

Driving up the Avenue that Tuesday morning, I noticed the old ladies still wore flowery housedresses and rested on their stoops with brooms in their hands. I wondered if they still baked bread. Probably, like May, only rarely. My great-aunt had been one of the last of the great household bakers. She'd make loaves all day Thursday, and I'd deliver them for her after school, collecting a quarter from each customer.

The Avenue, the main drag between the South Shawnee rail complex and my neighborhood, was still lined with narrow brick row houses, two or three stories tall. I'd been born in one of them.

No, that's not true. I was really born in Shawnee City Hospital, where the wounded engineer had been taken. I was born premature, they tell me, and I was only moved into the row house when they let me out of the hospital incubator. A couple of years later, after my father was sent to Korea, my mother and I moved up the hill to share her father's house.

At the traffic light, I turned the corner where her father, my grandfather, had sometimes boarded what he never stopped calling "the streetcar." It took him to his job repairing railroad cars in the South Shawnee shops.

A short distance up the grade, I turned right again, into the alley, steering the Ford past a few small backyards until I reached my own. I pulled out of the alley and into my parking place. I climbed out from behind the wheel and gave the car a pat for its good work.

Tattoo gave a right-handed wave to old Daniel, who was already out on his porch for the day. Then we hiked up the hill toward our common back porch.

"You want to come in for coffee?" he asked me. "May might take pity on you and feed you some breakfast."

He was always offering me breakfast, or ice cream, or dinner. Maybe he thought I was too skinny. Or maybe it was just the way the old people had of making food a communal event, of always wanting to feed you a piece of cake or a cookie. It had been so all my life.

"No, I've got a pot full at home. There's a woman coming to pick up a passport picture sometime today. And I better get these negatives started for the paper," I said.

We split up at the porch, him going left and up his steps, me heading right and up mine. I began feeling guilty about turning him down twice in a row. Just before he went in his door, I called, "How about breakfast tomorrow? Can you swing that?"

"Possible probable," he said in a gruff put-on voice. "If you ain't over by nine, I'll rise you up."

He obviously knew my sleeping habits.

I was sitting in the front room at the scratched-up table I used for a desk, writing a letter to send with my next batch of photos to the railroad magazine, when she rang the bell.

She was wearing a trench coat, or whatever the female version of a trench coat is called. It made her look even more businesslike than the matching skirt and jacket of Monday.

"Are my photos ready?" she asked.

"Yeah."

I picked up an envelope from the table and handed it to her. She opened the flap carefully, as if she were dreading it, and took out the prints. Tilting each one toward and away from the light, she looked them over slowly, as customers often do when they're studying themselves trapped on paper.

"I imagine they look like me," she finally said.

"You look better in person, but they're not bad. You're just a little nervous around the mouth."

"They could be worse. How much do I owe you?"

"Pick the one you want. For a photo I usually charge—"

She cut me off. "I'll take them all."

Good deal. I needed more customers like her.

I told her the grand total and she placed her handbag on the table, took out her billfold, and counted out the cash.

"How does one stop being 'a little nervous around the mouth' in photographs?" she asked as she put the photos and her billfold back in her purse.

"I suppose by losing the fear that many people have of the camera. And by seeing yourself look good in a photo for a change."

"How does one go about losing the fear of the camera?" she asked, glancing at me as she closed her purse. All those "one"'s she used made it seem as if she were speaking about someone else.

"You could get your picture taken more often." I laughed. I sounded like a salesman.

She never cracked a smile. "Can you take some more now?"

"Sure, that's what I do."

Without another word, she led me back to the studio. There, she put her bag on the floor by the wall and took off her coat. After searching for a clean place to stow it, she simply dropped it on top of her purse.

I was amazed how different she looked now than she had the morning before. No longer the prim businesswoman, she was costumed like a girl. But not like a modern girl. Like a Victorian one almost. No wonder she'd come in wearing the trench coat.

She was wearing a white dress that ended just below her knee. The loose top disguised her bustline. Above her breasts and at her wrists was lace. Her stockings were a sheer white, allowing the flesh of her legs to shine through just a little. She had on flat silvery slippers. Her makeup, too, was lighter, almost nonexistent, though there was a sort of silver sheen around her green eyes.

She reached up and brushed her hand through her hair so it fluffed a little and appeared less perfect. Looking slightly embarrassed, she said, "I always seem so hard and angular in pictures. I wanted to try something else."

"You're paying," I said. "It's your business. Some people dress up like cowboys and saloon girls and get their pictures snapped in a booth at the beach. If you ask me, this is much classier."

"Can you get all of me in?" she asked, ignoring my comments.

I looked through the camera. "As long as you stay around the stool at that end of the room."

She slid up on the stool and turned to her left a bit. She knew her best side.

"Stop worrying about the camera," I said as I lined up the shot. "Just forget it. You know what you want to look like. Just act it out. Choose a position, an angle, where you feel comfortable, in control. Don't be afraid to smile or move or throw your head back or anything else. Movement takes the self-consciousness out of it."

While she was looking my way, I clicked the first picture. I knew right off she wasn't ready. The moment she saw me move, her slight embarrassment had become outright camera shyness.

"Don't flinch," I said. "Remember, you want a picture of yourself. Help me out."

"Can't I be the one to say 'Cheese'?" she asked distantly. "Can't I tell you when to do it?"

"Sure," I said, realizing immediately it was a game I might be able to use again.

She looked to her left again, showing off her profile. Settling herself silently, she rested her hands in the lap of the white skirt and modestly crossed her ankles.

"Now," she softly instructed after a minute or so. "Take my picture now."

Click.

"Again."

Click.

Without budging her body, she tilted her head toward me,

lifted her chin high, and flashed me a smile that was close to the wise, almost cynical one she'd first showed me the morning before.

"Now."

Click.

Lowering her chin and positioning her mouth into something of a pout, she almost commanded, "Now."

Click.

Then she gently slid off the stool and stood beside it, her right hand resting on the seat. She crossed her right ankle lazily in front of her left.

"Now."

Click.

Another minute went by while she stood there, obviously figuring out what to do next. Then, moving into action, she crouched down behind the stool. Her hands gripping the rungs, she said, "Now."

Click.

She poked her head out from behind the left side of the stool.

"Now."

Click.

Playing hide-and-seek, she moved her head behind the stool once more and then inched it out on the right side.

"Now."

Click.

She stood up and climbed back on the stool slowly, balancing herself so she could raise her heels to the seat. The white skirt slid playfully up her thighs. She put her pale arms around her white-stockinged legs and pulled them tightly toward her.

"Now."

Click.

"Again."

Click.

She lowered her legs and stared spacily in my direction for an instant. Then she squirmed on the wooden seat, adjusting her legs until they were hanging down on either side of the stool.

Facing me head-on, she said, "Now."

Click.

She began swinging her legs, like a bored little girl, swinging them higher each time, higher and higher, until she was kicking like a cancan dancer, bad little girl in white, lips separated so that her white teeth showed.

"Now."

Click.

Kicking higher and higher, her bare thighs flashing with each kick.

"Now, Jack Reese."

Click.

"Again."

Click.

She stopped kicking, stopped moving altogether, and fell into an almost meditative calm. Eventually she climbed off the stool and picked up her coat.

"I'll be back for my pictures tomorrow," she said as she covered her costume with the trench coat.

She reached for her pocketbook and left.

I stood behind the camera, confused.

··· 5 ···

I was still asleep when the phone rang Wednesday morning.
How many times the thing had rung, I had no idea. The sound
had begun somewhere deep down in my dream, like a fading
ambulance siren or a distant fire alarm.

"You coming over for breakfast or not?" Tattoo growled after
I'd managed to struggle down the steps to the phone.

"On my way," I mumbled.

Back upstairs, I put on the uniform I'd worn all fall—khaki
pants and a flannel shirt. I hurried down to the kitchen and into
the bathroom to splash water on my face, brush my teeth, and
run a comb through my hair. I stared at the face reflected in the
mirror. I looked almost awake. No better, no worse-looking
than usual.

Then I went out my back door and walked around to Tattoo's, going inside the kitchen after I'd given a hard rap to announce myself.

He was puttering around with coffee cups and May was heft-
ing a heavy iron skillet, about to pour bacon grease in a can.

"Knew I'd have to call you," he said, handing me a cup before
I even sat down.

"That's what phones are for, I guess." At least that was why I had one, though like the old Ford I could scarcely afford it. Modern conveniences cost a bundle.

I sipped at the coffee and felt my head begin to clear as soon as the liquid slid down my throat.

"Were you up late?" asked May as she cracked an egg on the edge of the skillet and artfully dropped the insides onto the hot black iron. The orange yoke remained unbroken and bravely rounded, not like some of the things I do to eggs. "You want one or two?"

"Two eggs. Yeah, I was up a lot of the night. I ended up walking around downtown for hours after I delivered my pictures to *The News*. When I got back, I couldn't sleep, so I worked in the darkroom a while."

"Something special?" she asked.

"No," I answered, deciding not to tell her about the woman in the trench coat.

"Downtown's not the same as it used to be, is it?" She carefully flipped over one of the eggs in the skillet. "It's downright sad down there."

I took another sip of coffee. "It's surely not the same as when I was growing up, when my mother worked at Levine's."

"Levine's is long gone," Tattoo said grumpily, pouring himself another cup of what he often called "mocha java." He filled mine to the top again. "All the stores that didn't close up altogether moved out to the shopping center ten years ago. You can hardly buy a pair of shoelaces."

"They asked me if I wanted to work in the store at the shopping center when the drugstore closed two years ago," said May. "I told them I was old enough to retire and get my Social Security. I worked in that store downtown for over forty years. Didn't want to have to worry how I'd get out to the shopping center every day. It's hard enough to get out there to market once a week."

She lifted the skillet and brought it over to the table. With a metal spatula, she placed two perfect overlight eggs on my plate beside four strips of bacon. Then she put eggs on Tattoo's plate and her own. Tattoo spread butter on the last two pieces of hot toast and handed them out.

"It really is hard on people now that all the corner groceries are closed," said May, sitting down. "I don't know what we'd do without you and your car. Can't walk any place anymore. I used to like to walk. Your mother and me'd have a good old time jabbering about our day when we'd walk home together."

"I remember."

I could still picture her stocky body moving up the long hill of Thomas Street after the downtown stores closed at five o'clock. Sometimes I'd meet my mother and her at Bernhardt's, at the corner of our street and the Avenue. Bernhardt's stayed open until six so people could buy groceries on their way home from work. My aunt worked behind the counter and filled in as butcher when Bernhardt was on a drunk. Sometimes I'd earn movie money by stocking cans on the high narrow shelves or filling up the bins of kidney beans, rice, flour, fig newtons.

Christ, only thirty-four and already nostalgic.

"You're awful quiet this morning," said Tattoo between mouthfuls. "I guess you seen your picture on the front page of *The News?*"

"No. You got one?" I asked.

May turned her thick body and grabbed the paper off the cupboard behind her. There at the top of the front page was the photo of the train wreck that Metling had liked.

The evening before I'd spread my shots across his desk and waited for a response. "Pretty good," he'd finally said, which was heavy praise from him. Only about forty, he had the cranky manner of a newspaperman who'd been at it a long time and wasn't easily impressed. "I like the one with the truck hanging in the air. I'll see you get a few extra dollars for running out there."

"The story ain't good, though," said Tattoo, rapping the page with his index finger.

ENGINEER INJURED IN DERAILMENT read the headline. According to *The News*, the engineer—one Harry Bryson, age thirty-one—was in stable condition at Shawnee City Hospital. The information was sketchy at best. Maybe that's how Metling had intended it. Bryson's injuries weren't spelled out. Nor was the cause of the accident, which was said to be under investigation by Shawnee–Potomac authorities.

"That's the last we'll hear of that story," proclaimed Tattoo.

"You know him—Harry Bryson?" I asked.

"I know the family. Used to work with his daddy."

"His mother worked awhile at the drugstore with me," said May.

"Any idea how seriously he's hurt?"

"He's lost a leg," said Tattoo.

I looked across the table at him. Him, with his arm missing from another railroad accident. I didn't know what to say and he volunteered nothing further.

"You going to be working full-time now for the newspaper?" May asked me.

"I don't plan to. No one's asked me to. Metling only calls when he can't get one of his staffers to do a job. I get most of the junk work. Last night he gave me an assignment I really don't want."

"What's that?"

"Hell, tomorrow night I'm supposed to get a picture of some preachers giving an award to their favorite congressman, Charles Whitford Canley."

"Son of a bitch, just like his daddy was. They kiss rich asses and hand the job down, father to son."

"Someone votes for them, Henry," said May. She always refused to call him Tattoo.

"You don't have to complain to me," I said. "I don't want to do it, but I don't know how to get out of it, short of putting myself out of any future jobs with *The News*. My grandfather's probably screaming at me from his grave."

"Why's a picture of Canley and some preachers have to be in the paper anyways?" asked Tattoo.

"Metling had mixed feelings, he said, but he guessed it was news," I answered.

"I told you about that paper! All them politicalized preachers ain't nothing but Sadducees and Pharisees like in the Bible. Those Billy-Sunday boys used to preach against the union like we was godless heathens. They probably still do."

"God knows the good preachers from the bum ones," said May.

"I hope he can tell the difference," said Tattoo.

"Reverend Ruffing's a good man," she said.

"He's all right," admitted Tattoo.

Reverend Ruffing was the pastor at the Methodist Church down the street where May went each Sunday morning, where I'd gone as a kid.

"He's started a food bank to help out-of-work people," she said.

"Somebody's got to help them," said Tattoo. "What's the president done but toss out a little cheese and butter that the taxpayer's already paid for?"

I recalled the long lines of people waiting for cheese and butter outside the handout center, which had once been the biggest movie theater downtown. The theater lobby had become a registration room, while the aisles contained boxes of surplus dairy products. I'd clicked my pictures of the line from the other side of the street, not really wanting to show faces in close-up, but only to show the scope of the hard times. Once a line like that would have been waiting to see a CinemaScope blockbuster. Now it was waiting for charity.

"We're lucky we all ain't back in sweatshops," said Tattoo angrily. "These young guys that work for the railroad now, they don't remember. They all voted 'servative 'cause they liked all that talk of cutting taxes. But whose taxes got cut? The big shots. Those boys don't remember the old battles. They think there always was decent wages and benefits, since there has been as long as they been around. Well, it's all ending. Look at Shawnee Steel, all those men who worked there all their lives out of work. And what do they tell them? Go to computer school. There's plenty of jobs in *The Washington Post*. There's lots of service jobs. *Service jobs*, they call them. I call them servants."

"Calm down, Henry," said May, staring across the table at the man she'd lived with for thirty-five years. "You're retired now. God is good."

"Yeah, they can't take the railroad retirement or the Social Security or the Medicare away. They can call Roosevelt the devil all they want and blame him for everything that's gone wrong for fifty years, but where would we be without him? He wasn't just no tinman with an actor's voice. FDR had a heart. He didn't make men waitresses. He put them to work building power dams and making parks. What if he hadn't started Social Security and the farmer subsidies that paid for all them goddamn five-pound hunks of cheese? And Eleanor, they make fun of her, but she'd go all over helping people. She'd go to coal towns and square dance with the miners at night. We ain't got no one like them no more. Instead, we got flag-wavers dressed in evening gowns standing in pulpits."

As his face grew redder and his voice got louder, I felt crummier and crummier that I'd let Metling con me into taking a picture of Congressman Charles Whitford Canley getting patted on the ass by a group of ministers.

When I got the chance, I said my good-byes and went next door.

··· 6 ···

I'd just about given up on her.

The streetlights were on and it was almost completely dark. I figured she wasn't coming.

Waiting for her, I'd whittled away the afternoon. For a while I'd sat on the front porch, but I'd gone inside when all the school kids started pouring down the hill like gutter water in flood season, with all their horseplay and clatter and their contagious happiness about being out of prison for the rest of the day. It just hadn't fit my mood.

Inside, I'd spent a good hour trying to straighten up my desk and the clutter of the front room to make it more presentable to her . . . and to other customers.

Waiting, I'd looked again through the photos of her in the white little-girl costume. For a moment, I'd felt a little like Charles Lutwidge Dodgson, alias Lewis Carroll. Aside from writing *Alice's Adventures in Wonderland* and *Through the Looking Glass*, that Victorian gentleman was known to dress up little girls and click their pictures in his studio at Christ Church.

I won't comment on his motives, but he wasn't a bad photographer. His girls often illustrated literary scenes. One was caped as Little Red Riding Hood, with no wolf in evidence. In another, Alice Pleasance Liddell, Carroll's inspiration for the famous Alice, was done up as "The Little Beggar Maid," ragged child of working-class English streets. The rags hardly clung to her shoulders, leaving her chest almost naked.

But, unlike Carroll, I was not fascinated by little girls. I'd dressed up no one. I'd merely hung out a shingle and she'd come to me, whoever she was.

Why? What kind of fantasy was she working out?

Shaking off the questions, I'd gone downstairs, cooked myself a couple of sausage-and-egg sandwiches, sat at the kitchen table a while, and flipped through the latest crop of magazines to see if I was missing any picture angles. Then I'd cleaned up my mess and stepped into the basement to sort through the negatives on the darkroom drying line.

When she finally showed up, she was wearing the same coat as the day before. She seemed slightly ill at ease as she looked through the prints of Tuesday's session. She stared a little longer at the one of her legs lifted high in the air. Then she hurriedly stuffed the photos in her purse, paid me my fee in cash, and stood there silently, like she was deciding what to do next.

"Are the pictures okay?" I asked, prodding her.

She nodded. Then she softly said, "You didn't give me the negatives. I'd like *all* my negatives, always."

"I'll be right back."

I went downstairs, pulled the negatives from the two sessions off the clothesline, slid them in a glassine envelope, and headed back upstairs.

She was no longer in the front room. "I'm back here," she called when she realized I didn't know where she was.

Again she surprised me.

She had taken off the trench coat and was standing on stiletto red heels in the middle of my studio.

She was wearing a pink dress.

Not just any pink, but the pinkest blushingest pink.

Not just any dress, but one of those sheeny tight-fitting ones with a low-cut top, straight out of the late fifties.

I was at a loss for words as I handed her the negatives, and simply stared at her new costume as she carefully bent down, her knees together, and placed the glassine envelope in her bag.

She couldn't help but notice my stare. "This dress was my mother's," she explained as she stood up. "I always liked clothes like this. They were made for women's bodies."

I chanced it. "It certainly looks like they were made for yours. . . . Who are you anyway?"

"Just a woman paying you to have her picture taken, as she wants it taken." There was no hint of nervousness in her voice. "Don't ask any more questions. You do have film in your camera?"

"Always. I take one roll out and put another in."

Her tongue flicked out to wet her shiny red lips and her green eyes grew serious beneath the dark eye shadow and long lashes. "Let's not waste time then."

"Whatever you say."

I went over to the tripod, adjusted lights, and began to slowly focus the camera while she turned away, stepped to the stool, and positioned herself on the edge of the seat, her thin red heels jabbing into the threadbare carpet. Her costume was perfect in every detail, right down to the seamed stockings. Had she found those in her mother's closet, too?

"Aren't you ready?" she asked, tenseness starting to creep into her voice.

"Yeah. Tell me when."

"Now."

Click.

She slid up onto the stool and crossed her legs inside the

tight skirt. Looking straight at the camera, with not a glimmer of softness or smile, she said, "Now."

Click.

She moved a little so that what she believed was her good side was in profile. Her skirt rode above her knee when she moved.

"Now."

Click.

She raised her right arm so that her long red fingernails rested gently against her powdered and rouged right cheek. Light reflected from the large bracelet on her thin wrist. Whether the bracelet was real or costume, hers or her mother's, it went well with the dress, as did the long glittering earrings.

"Take it now."

Click.

"Again."

Click.

Holding down her skirt, she slid off the stool and moved behind it, folded her hands, and calmly positioned them on the seat in front of her.

"Now."

Click.

She leaned forward so that her elbows rested on the seat.

"Now."

Click.

Her breasts swelled out from the top of the pink dress.

"Take it now."

Click.

With small steps, she walked around to the front of the stool, turned her back to me, and rather coyly stared over her bare shoulder toward the camera lens.

"Take it now."

Click.

She turned once more and carelessly slid up onto the stool, her skirt rising high on her thighs, the dark rings at the top of her stockings showing.

"Take it now."

Click.

She hooked her high heels behind a stool rung, her knees moving apart.

"Now."

Click.

For a long moment, she seemed lost in her thoughts, in her fantasies. Then she reached behind her, her breasts pushing forward with the action, and unzipped the dress, letting the top of it fall toward her waist. A sheer pink strapless bra held back her breasts.

"Take it now."

Click.

She slid off the stool and pushed the tight dress down to her ankles. A lacy pink half-slip covered her from waist to knee. As she lifted her right leg to step out of the dress, she said, "Take it."

Click.

She bent down, her breasts almost tumbling out of her pink brassiere, and tossed the dress on top of her coat and purse. Then she slid the slip off, added it to the pile, and turned back to face the camera.

"Take me now."

Click.

She reached up and fluffed her brown hair. She stood so that her legs made an inverted V and put her hands on her waist, on the elastic waistband of pink lingerie-catalog underpants, slit open at the sides. *Her mother's?*

"Take me now."

Click.

Sitting on the stool again, she angled her body to the left, crossing her legs so that the slit underpants fell open at the side. The black strap of her garterbelt stretched across her white thigh.

"Take me now."

Click.

Moving again, she slid off the stool and turned her back to me, bent her leg at the knee, and glanced over her shoulder and then down at her calf, as if to see if the fine black line of the seam was straight. The stockings were so sheer that only the seams and the dark rings around her white thighs gave away the fact she wasn't barelegged.

"Take me now."

Click.

Reaching behind her, she slid down the slitted panties so her buttock showed, her upper thighs white against the black garter strap.

"Now."

Click.

She turned to face front. Her long thin fingers pushed the right side of her panties to the left, exposing just the slightest curl of dark brown pubic hair. She slid her red-nailed fingers inside the silk.

"Take me now."

Click.

"Take me again."

The camera wouldn't click.

I tried again. No luck.

"I've got to change film," I told her.

As I rewound the roll, she stood in place, her hand inside her panties, eyes closed, legs apart, swaying on her high red heels.

I took the first roll out and hurried to put another in, not wanting to break her mood, not wanting her to stop. But I was either too slow or she had second thoughts. From across the room, I could almost feel her relax.

Opening her eyes, she asked, "Where's your bathroom?"

"Downstairs, off the kitchen."

She picked up her slip, her dress, her coat, and her purse and almost ran from the room. The sound of her heels grew more distant, until I heard the bathroom door close.

Feeling a little weak, I crossed the room and sat on the stool, waiting for her to come back. Finally, I heard the bathroom door open, then footsteps cross the kitchen linoleum. Then the back door opened and closed.

I didn't react for a minute, but eventually I stood up and ran down the steps and out the kitchen door and down the hilly backyard toward the alley.

I couldn't see anyone.

She'd certainly disappeared fast enough. Either she knew the alley as well as I did, or she had a car nearby. Or she could fly.

I stared up the alley toward old Daniel's porch, wondering if he was sitting there alone in the dark, if he'd seen her run by, if he could tell me the direction she had fled. But he wasn't outside. The downstairs lights were on inside his square two-story frame house. He was probably watching TV or doing whatever old men do at night.

Just as well. I didn't want to have to explain anything to him. I hadn't mentioned her to Tattoo either, except to say I was making a passport photo for a woman.

Passport photo. Was she really going off to some exotic land, or had that just been to check me out? I was fairly sure I knew the answer.

I was also sure she'd be back. Without a doubt. She'd been careful not to leave any of the first batch of negatives. She wouldn't think of leaving behind tonight's.

I paused for a moment and pondered it. If she weren't so

damn serious, it could almost have been funny. Then again, perhaps a whole new field of endeavor was opening up for me. I could change my sign:

SPECIALIST IN CAPTURING FANTASIES
Come as you are, or as you would be

A car turned into the alley, its headlights swinging with the turning vehicle until they were shooting straight down the much patched and potholed lane. I watched it come closer and closer, not realizing until it was even with me that it was a police car cruising on night patrol. The cop looked my way as he drove by.

So they still did that.

When I was a kid, a police car had come down the alley nearly every night shortly after ten o'clock, the city curfew for kids under sixteen. Summer nights we'd still be out playing at ten, so when the cop came through we'd scurry into backyards or slide into dark garages through holes in the rusting metal walls. When the cop was gone, we'd get back to jailbreak, our nighttime game.

The neighborhood was younger then and there were more kids. We'd divide up into two teams—the crooks and the cops. The crooks would hide under porches or in shadowed crevices and the cops would fan out to find them. The streetlight pole was the jail. Once caught, you'd stand next to it and hope another crook would creep into the circle of light and tag you free.

Being a crook was always more fun than being a cop. My punkier impulses must trace back to those alley nights. The hiding and the breaking out were always more exciting than the finding and putting into jail.

In our imaginations we would disappear into the night, never to be found.

Like she had.

Who would have believed such a job would come my way in Shawnee? How could I begin to tell the old men about her?

Crazy, but they just might understand.

Tattoo, who'd worn a picture of a sensuous woman on an arm he'd once possessed.

Daniel, who'd told me how he'd paid a friend a dollar to introduce him to his wife-to-be in 1924, flapper days.

The old men admired pretty legs and valued the feel of cock in cunt as much as any other sensation in life.

"I've lived a hell of a long time and yet I've only learnt much about two things," Daniel had told me one hot afternoon. "Railroading and fucking."

Railroading & Fucking. As good a working title for my photo book as I was likely to find.

I'd put her in the book if I ever got it together. She was now part of Shawnee 1982 to me. Besides, the thing would be easier to sell with a spread of her in it.

Put a blond wig on her head and, with that low-cut pink dress, she might pass for Marilyn Monroe.

We could find a grate down by the abandoned passenger station some night and restage the famous scene from *The Seven Year Itch.*

She would stand over the grate and let the warm air blow up between her thighs and waft her skirt up above her waist. She would slam her hands toward her crotch to hold the skirt down in front while the rest of it floated above her thighs.

I smiled. Her fantasies were causing me to have fantasies. They were catching.

It was getting late and chilly. I went back inside to the darkroom.

··· 7 ···

Weird.

Monday morning she had seemed so dress-for-success proper.

Tuesday's child had been a more provocative one.

Wednesday night she had played dress up—or down—slipping into her mother's clothes and high heels. Her mother must have been a dazzler in her prime.

Thursday's child hadn't come.

Unless she'd appeared during the time I'd been clicking Canley and the evangelists. Quite a different job than hers.

Metling had promised me the whole thing would take less than an hour, and it had. I'd driven to the church, snapped the pictures, delivered the film for *The News'* darkroom to process, and been home before eight o'clock.

It had been the only time I'd been away from the house all day, and it must have been when she'd come by. If she'd come at all. Maybe she'd had second thoughts. Maybe she was backing off, afraid of what might happen when she again stepped into my parlor and shed her trench coat.

Her costumes seemed important somehow, maybe because I knew so little else about her. Not even her name. I knew nothing except her fantasies. And though I was getting sucked into them, they were *her* fantasies, not mine.

What she wore was my only clue to what was going on inside her.

Weird to see a woman's fantasy but to know nothing of her reality.

She could be a market clerk for all I knew.

When she hadn't come by 11:15, I gave up on her and for once went to bed at a decent hour, determined not to wait around the next day. I thought I'd get up early and make my way out to the South Shawnee switchyards to catch the trains moving through the soft morning mist before the sun burned it away and turned the light hard. Morning was usually a good time to click frames in mountain light. Even as a kid, I'd appreciated the look of the foggy patches hunching over the ridges surrounding Shawnee.

Adjusting May's quilt over me, I decided that if all else failed, I might try marketing some scenics.

Hell, Metling might even buy a scenic to break up his gray column pages.

Lying there, I mentally kicked myself for missing her, if indeed I had. A session with her would certainly have been more entertaining, even more profitable, than the visit to the Shawnee Independent Bible Church.

The Reverend Richard Baum had come over to greet me as soon as I'd stepped into the church basement. "Are you the photographer from *The News*?" he'd asked in a genial-enough voice, extending his hand. He was wearing one of those slick pastel suits that come unslicked by the end of a hard day. It looked like his day hadn't been too hard.

"I'm the photographer," I answered.

"We're just about ready for you."

He led me toward a U-shaped arrangement of folding tables where about twenty people were seated. The room was a long rectangle with cheap paneling and a drop ceiling. They probably held Sunday school in it as well as church dinners. Three or four older women were scurrying around, clearing plain white dishes from the tables. The plates showed the remains of fried chicken and mashed potatoes.

"Would you like coffee or something?" asked Baum, motioning for me to sit on a folding chair.

"No, thanks. I've eaten."

Feeling out of place, I waited quietly. Once the ladies had finished clearing the plates, Reverend Baum stood up and announced in a strong clear voice, "We've had a successful conversation with the congressman this evening. We're glad he was able to take time from his busy schedule to break bread with us. Soon he must go on to another event, so we'll be postponing dessert for a few minutes while we present him with a token of our appreciation for his efforts in Congress over the years."

Next to Baum, a middle-aged woman in a pale pink high-necked dress reached beneath the table and handed him an octagonal piece of wood upon which was mounted a bronze-colored plaque.

Displaying the plaque to the others, Baum said, "As you are aware, Congressman Charles Whitford Canley has long been a staunch supporter of the Christian American Way. He has sponsored legislation to put prayer back into this nation's public schools. He has opposed abortion. He has backed our beloved president in his various tax-cut measures. He has been an ardent foe of International Communism and of creeping socialism at home. Early in his political career, he stood up to the critics of the Vietnam War. I could speak all night about his brave efforts, from his campaign against pornography to his valiant words concerning the leftist anti-nuclear movement. He stands, in short, for a return to the basic Christian values that made this country great. Many organizations have recognized his dedication and his patriotism. Last week in Washington, the Daughters of the American Revolution paid tribute to him. We members of the Bible Ministers of Shawnee offer him this modest plaque, and our continued support."

Congressman Canley, a tall man in his forties, rose, took his award from Baum, gave a forgettable acceptance speech, and then thanked the group. I snapped a photo of him looking down at the plaque as he talked.

Then all the preachers crowded around to congratulate him and shake his hand. Baum put them in some sort of order and I took a couple photos of the group. Ignoring Baum's directions, one preacher, a big red-haired man about my age, reached over, tapped Canley on the back and crowded closer to him, not wanting to be missed. Even preachers like Baum had their problems with rank.

Soon after, Canley headed for the door. I was about to follow when Baum cut me off.

"Thanks for coming," he said softly. "You're welcome to stay for pie."

"I've got to get my film down to the office."

"You might want this," he said, offering me a slip of paper. "My wife wrote down the names of the clergymen in the group picture."

I took the paper from him. "Sorry, I should have done it myself."

"No trouble," he said, like the best of public relations men.

And that's all there was to it.

The phone rang.

I tossed back the quilt, climbed out of bed, and almost stumbled down the steps, having no idea what time it was or how long I'd managed to sleep.

"Are my photos ready?"

"Wait a minute. I'm half asleep. Who is this?"

Of course, even half asleep, I knew who it was.

"I stopped by for my pictures tonight and you weren't there," she said, a sad, stood-up inflection to her voice.

"Ah, the lady in pink."

"Don't make fun of me," she said. "I'm a customer, aren't I?"

"I'm sorry . . . you're right. What time is it, anyway?"

"Around midnight. I imagined you'd still be awake."

"Well, I am now, sort of."

"Where were you?" she asked, almost as if she was jealous.

"I had another job. I'd have told you last night if you hadn't sneaked out the back door. I'd have called you if I knew who you were."

She ignored what I'd said. "Is it all right for me to come over now?"

"Now?"

"I can't sleep. I want my pictures . . . and . . ."

"And what?"

She didn't answer, just left a long silence for me to take in as I stood there in my underwear in the darkness of the front room.

"Where are you now?" I asked.

"At home."

"Where's that?"

"I'll be there in less than an hour," she said quickly, before hanging up.

It was all getting weirder and weirder. Our next session would be in the middle of the night. There was no sense trying to guess what Thursday's child would be like. She'd arrive soon enough.

··· 8 ···

She kept me waiting.

Sitting at the desk in the front room, I felt like writing her a time-and-a-half bill for the waiting she'd put me through, and for the late-night duty.

I drained a mug of coffee, then a second, and headed back downstairs for a third. It was already after one o'clock. If I was going to be up all night, I might as well really be up all night. After she left, I would hike across town and hit the South Shawnee switchyards at dawn—before the caffeine ran out and I crashed.

I poured the mug full, put the coffeepot down on the stove, walked to the back door, and stared out the glass toward the alley. To the left of the sheet-metal garages flashed a jagged scarlet-and-yellow.

I just about threw the mug on the table. I pulled open the door and ran down the yard yelling "Fire! Fire! Fire!" as loudly as I could, hoping I would wake up the whole goddamn neighborhood.

I ran around my Ford, jumped down into the alley, and rammed my knee into the back of a parked car that I hadn't expected to be there. Backing away from the car, I stepped in a pothole. My ankle twisted, my bruised knee gave out, and I fell on the ragged roadway.

"Fire! Fire! Fire!" I screamed.

I grabbed the bumper of the car and pulled myself to my feet. My ankle ached. Unable to run, I limped toward Daniel's house.

"Fire! Fire! Fire!"

The intense heat of the flaming house kept me at a distance. The porch where the old man had passed so much of his time was burning like crumpled paper. Flames showed in every window of the two-story structure. Fire slithered up the outside wooden walls. The roof crackled like kindling. Sparks were carried by the night breeze and landed like glowing match tips on the tin garage roofs nearby.

Despite the flames and heat, I debated whether I should dash inside and try to find Daniel.

"We got to move that car before the fire engines come," said Tattoo, suddenly beside me.

"Shouldn't we try to save him?"

"Are you crazy? Look at that house a-burning! There's no way to get inside it. It's too late for him anyway. All we can do is keep the thing from spreading. May was calling the fire department when I run down. We got to move that son-of-a-bitching car so the damn fire trucks can come up the alley."

He was trying to sound reasonable, but I could tell he was as agitated as I was. He'd known Daniel for a long time.

"Come on," he ordered. "The siren's already blowing. Can't you hear it?"

The fire, the sparks in the darkness, the pain in my knee and ankle . . . I wasn't sure what I could hear.

Tattoo started walking toward the parked car and I followed him. "Parked" is generous. The driver of the blue Volkswagen had made no apparent effort to move the vehicle out of the middle of the alley between my yard and Daniel's burning house. He'd just left it there.

Tattoo opened the car door and peered in. "The keys are in it." Watching me approach, he asked, "What happened to your leg?"

"I ran into this son-of-a-bitching thing and twisted my ankle," I said, borrowing his words.

"And you wanted to run in that house after Daniel? You really are crazy. If you want to do something, then drive this German monstrosity down the alley and out of the way."

Nodding, I climbed into the VW and turned the key in the ignition. The car started right up, as if the engine was still hot. I slipped the stick shift into first and began crawling ahead. I had to go forward, past the fire, or else I would have risked bottlenecking the fire trucks. I gassed the car hard as I neared the burning house, wanting to get by as quickly as possible, my head filled with visions of the sparks in the narrow alley somehow finding a way to ignite the gas tank.

When I figured I was out of danger, I let up on the accelerator and tried to calm myself. I drove most of the way down the alley until I found a place that was broad enough to park and still let a fire truck by if need be. I left the keys in the ignition and climbed out, my leg almost collapsing again when I put weight on it.

I limped to the back of the car and studied it. It had in-state license plates. I didn't remember seeing it in the neighborhood before, but that wasn't unusual. Cars weren't something I spent a lot of time noticing.

Slowly I made my way back up the alley toward the fire. The whole block seemed awake by then. Light bulbs burned in every bedroom. The night was filled with voices coming from all directions, people on back porches, people rushing through their yards to the alley. A crowd had formed a semicircle around the front of Daniel's flame-defeated home.

I pushed my way through the people until I found Tattoo. Soon a bathrobe-clad May joined us. She handed Tattoo a brown sweater to put on over his white T-shirt.

The house had started to collapse in on itself by the time the fire engines arrived. There was little the firemen could do. Some of them fought to extinguish the bed of glowing coals in what had once been the center of the dwelling. Others wetted down nearby buildings and garages, which sizzled and steamed when the water hit the red-hot metal.

The alley took on a glary, surrealistic tone, like a wartime London street after a Nazi bombing or a disastrous rock festival in the midst of its last night. Neighbors stood around in robes, nightclothes, even wrapped in blankets. The firemen, in full gear, ran back and forth. The garish streetlights, the dying flames, the smoke and steam, the swirling fire engine lights . . . nothing seemed real any longer.

A city cop and a man with a State Fire Marshal emblem on his shirt moved through the crowd, ordered us to step further back, and asked if anybody knew anything about what had happened.

When they got to us, I told them how I'd been in my kitchen looking out the back door and seen the flames and run down and tried to wake people up and moved the car. They coolly wrote it all down, each keeping his own set of notes. Then they headed toward the fire chief.

I glanced over at Tattoo. The strangeness of the light in the alley gave his face a dark cast that would have seemed menacingly demonic if I hadn't known it was caused by sadness and sorrow.

"What do we do now?" I asked.

"I suppose we bury Daniel, if there's anything left to bury," he said.

He seemed older to me right then than he ever had before. Under his brown sweater, his usually broad shoulders looked hunched and his strong chest seemed caved in.

After a while, he reached for May's arm and led her home.

··· 9 ···

"Where's the pictures?" Metling asked.

It was Friday afternoon, about four-thirty.

"Of what?" I asked back, still groggy. I'd been asleep when the phone rang—and only for three or four hours. Getting to sleep had been an obstacle.

"The photos of the fire," he said, but he sounded like he meant "The photos of the fire, *stupid*."

"I didn't take any."

"It was in your neighborhood, wasn't it? Didn't you get any shots at all? I figured you'd be down here with prints long ago."

"I was too busy."

"You were the one who spotted the fire, weren't you? How many Jack Reeses live up there? When you get down here, I want you to talk to a reporter. It's arson, you know. *It's murder.*"

"Christ, I don't want to talk to a reporter," I said.

"We can talk later," Metling shot back. "You get out and snap some pictures of what's left of the house or something. Get your film down here. We'll take care of developing it, like we did the roll of Canley last night."

Canley last night.

Was that just last night? My world had changed a couple times since.

Metling hung up and, though I hated doing it, I got dressed and went down to the alley. With a miserable feeling in my stomach, I stood in front of the pile of charred rubble that had once been old Daniel's home. I aimed the camera at the darkest, blackest, most burnt goddamned area. If Metling wanted a photo of the fire, then the uglier the picture, the better. I clicked five or six shots of the same thing, then climbed into the Ford and headed downtown.

It was turning dark by the time I got back to the alley. My headlights picked up on someone standing, staring, at the destroyed house.

The person turned toward me. From his odd gait, his leaning slightly forward and to the side to balance a missing left arm, I knew who it was.

"Where you been?" Tattoo asked when I climbed out of the car.

"At *The News* office."

"What do they know? What'd the police tell them?" he asked.

"It's murder. Arson. I didn't get the details. I didn't feel like waiting around. Just handed my film to a girl at the front desk and left."

"I'll get the son of a bitch that killed Daniel," he said. "You know that goddamn foreign car's still parked down the alley. Are the cops looking into it?"

"I don't know. If it's still there, it must be all right. You heard me tell the police and the fire marshal about it."

We began walking up the hill to the house.

"You had supper yet?" asked Tattoo.

"No."

"Come on in," he offered.

Dinner was a wordless affair. Like the neighborhood around us, we seemed to have sunk into silence in the wake of the fire.

Sitting at the table, picking at a hunk of May's Poorman's Cake, I knew Saturday morning's paper would break the silence. The fire, the murder, had happened too late for *The News'* Friday edition, but judging from the urgency with which Metling had wanted a picture of Daniel's house, I knew there'd be a big spread the next day.

"When's Daniel going to be buried?" I asked.

"Sunday afternoon," Tattoo mumbled, without looking up from his cake.

"It's all supposed to be in tomorrow's paper," said May. "Reverend Ruffing's doing the service out at the cemetery. We're having a small reception here afterwards. Don't expect many. No one knows of any family left."

"He never had children, did he?"

"Not that anyone knows of."

"Sad way to end, ain't it?" said Tattoo. "With hardly a body left to bury and hardly a mourner left to see you out."

"Fires are nasty," I mumbled, realizing immediately how dumb it sounded.

"You're too young to remember the one in your house years ago," said May.

"I remember some hushes about it when I was a kid. What happened exactly?"

She slid her plate out of the way and rested her elbows on the table. "It was years before Henry and me lived here. I only know what your granddaddy and mother told me. It was back in the thirties, during Prohibition, when your mother was young. Your people was living in this side of the house and your grandfather was renting the other side out to a man who come into Shawnee from out in the mountains somewheres."

"Buck," inserted Tattoo.

"You want to tell it?" May asked him.

"No."

"Your family always felt something was strange over next door," she went on. "There'd be water running and bottles clinking at all hours. The fellow seemed to be taking out box loads of something late at night, and they'd hear his old Model T running up the hill someplace. Till one night there was a boom. Like an exploding gas tank or something. The fire swooped up the stairs from the basement before anybody knew what was going on. Your side of the house was just about gutted. Fire probably would've spread to this side too but for the brick wall between them."

She stopped, but I didn't want her to.

"Wasn't there someone killed?" I asked. "I thought someone died and that's why they never talked much about it."

"A thirteen-year-old girl. The bootlegger's daughter," answered May. "She was asleep upstairs and couldn't get down the steps and no one could get up through the flames."

"Named Mary," added Tattoo. "You ain't seen her ghost over there, have you?"

May shot him a shut-up glance.

"Whatever became of them?" I asked.

"They moved," she said. "You know your granddaddy was a teetotaler. He was an upright man, even if he never went to church."

"Church ain't got nothing to do with morals," said Tattoo.

She ignored him. "I always heard they moved to somewhere in Shantytown, by the canal. I guess they set up another still there. Your people remodeled the other side of the house and liked it so much they moved over there."

"You ain't been making home brew in that darkroom of yours, have you?" asked Tattoo. "He had his still in that basement over there."

This time, May didn't object to his remark. We all laughed and some of the tension over Daniel was relieved for a while.

··· 10 ···

Daniel Morgan Jones, 84, of Baxter Street, Shawnee, died early Friday, October 15, in a fire at his residence.

Born November 11, 1897, in Wild Stream, West Virginia, he was the son of the late Albert M. and Susan Schmidt Jones.

Mr. Jones came to Shawnee in the early 1920s to work for the Shawnee–Potomac Railroad. He retired in 1963.

He was a veteran of World War I and a member of the United Brotherhood of Carmen. He was a Protestant.

He was preceded in death by his wife, Ella Scott Jones, in 1964. There are no known survivors.

Burial will be at Rose Garden Cemetery at 2:00 p.m. on Sunday, October 17, with the Rev. Joseph Ruffing officiating.

How neatly a man's life could be wrapped up in a few paragraphs.

I read the obituary again. Not so much as a hint of *Railroading & Fucking*, or the time in 1935 when Daniel said he'd almost killed a man, raising a wrench in hot-blood against another worker who'd claimed Uncle Joe Stalin was a finer man than Franklin Roosevelt.

The obit couldn't begin to explain him.

How he liked to tell of sitting under a tree in France when he got word of the armistice ending World War I. How the dough-boy beside him had been blown apart five minutes after the war was supposed to have ended.

How he fought his second war, walking the picket line with the United Brotherhood.

He was a Protestant. Sure he was. Just like my grandfather, Tat-too, and me.

I turned back to the front page of Saturday morning's *News.* There was the photo I'd taken of what had once been his home. The picture looked as gray, dark, and murky as I'd figured it would. No great advertisement for me as a photographer.

The story told how what was left of Daniel's body had been found by fire fighters near dawn on Friday, and how arson was suspected.

I was named as the person who first saw the blaze. Metling was probably still fuming that I hadn't loaded his reporter up with all the details.

At least only two of us knew why I was up at 1:00 A.M., looking down into the alley. It wasn't spread across the head-lines that I'd been waiting for a mystery woman.

Who hadn't come.

Hadn't come the night of the fire.

Hadn't come Friday, to my knowledge.

Hadn't yet come Saturday morning.

I hadn't heard a peep out of her since that crazy phone call. Her pictures from Wednesday night still sat on my desk.

I went down to the darkroom to pass some time. I figured, if she came, she'd see the note on the front door: *If no one answers, ring bell to darkroom.* But, as I puttered around, the bell didn't ring.

The darkroom seemed strange to me. May's story of the moonshiner and his still kept running through my mind, as it had the night before. Trying to sleep, I'd kept thinking of Daniel, and shaking off Daniel, I'd thought of the girl burned in the explosion. In the middle of the night, the rain had started, beating on the tin roof and adding to my sleep problems.

In temperamental October fashion, Saturday morning had been unseasonably warm, as if the fire at Daniel's were rising again to scorch the whole neighborhood.

Daniel.

I sorted through my negatives until I found the one of him sitting on his swing in August.

I made fresh chemicals and prepared to make a book-quality print.

I put the negative in the enlarger and focused, trying to judge the light and dark of it.

His face sucked me in.

There, in reverse image, the face black as if charred, the eyes burning, its shadows and wrinkled hollows ghost white.

What kind of bastard would kill him?

··· 11 ···

As he spoke the words he thought appropriate, I wondered how well Reverend Joe Ruffing had known Daniel Jones. The Bible verses he quoted seemed to have little to do with the old man.

Sunday's cold damp wind beat at us as we stood on top of the hill at Rose Garden Cemetery, not far from my own family's plot. It was one of those fierce fall winds that occasionally rise up to dry the mud.

The Reverend Ruffing talked in a soft monotone and I kept returning to Thursday night. To her call. To the flames I'd seen out the back door. To running down the hill, bumping into the car, twisting my ankle. To the feeling of guilt at not being able to do anything to save Daniel.

Those scenes stayed in my head the whole drive back to Tattoo and May's, and even as I reached down to the platter of little quartered sandwiches on the kitchen table.

"May's certainly gone to a lot of trouble for the few of us," said Joe Ruffing, reaching for a sandwich at the same time.

"She always does when food's involved. She loves messing around with hors d'oeuvres and cake decorating and all that fancy stuff. She missed her calling. She should have been a caterer," I said. "When I was a kid, she was always making these little sandwiches and frostinged cakes and sweet trifles whenever she or my mother had people over. I suppose she wanted to keep busy at something before the funeral."

"You've known May a long time, haven't you?" he asked.

"All my life. I grew up next door."

"She's filled me in about you," he said.

I looked down at the platter. Deciding against cheese salad, I picked up a ham salad sandwich. With my other hand I grabbed a cracker topped by a thin spread of cream cheese and a whole olive.

"She speaks highly of you," I said to him.

"I've noticed her husband doesn't bark at me anymore if I stop by."

"Tattoo's impressed by the food bank you started," I told him. "You're not likely to see him in the front pew, though."

"The food bank just came about. I saw the need and convinced some of the congregation to help. May's been one of the stalwarts. Somebody had to do something. There are a lot of people out of work, scrimping by on a few dollars a week, with no prospects for anything better. Back home, it's like that too."

"Where's back home?"

"Pittsburgh area. I grew up in a steel-mill neighborhood. It was basically a lot like here."

"How'd you get to be a preacher?"

"Went to seminary." He smiled before biting into another cream-cheese-and-olive cracker. "In seminary they always kidded me I was a social worker disguised as a minister. Take Daniel, for example. He didn't really belong to the church, but I met him last spring while I was walking up the alley. Later I called the Commission on Aging and asked if they'd deliver hot lunches to him."

"He told me about that."

"I assume they followed through."

"Over his objections."

"I guess I really shouldn't go around doing things like that," said Ruffing. "But I don't think I'm necessarily here so much to preach as I am to pastor."

"You sound out of touch with the theology of the eighties," I said. "Aren't you supposed to be laying a little guilt on people, or at least helping them realize that free-market economics and nuclear bombs are the flowering of the Gospel?"

"Jesus would overturn their tables," he said, his voice just as sarcastic as mine had been.

I looked him over closely as he picked up another sandwich. A tall bachelor, his black suit hung on his bones like a shirt on a clothes hanger, making me feel hale and hearty. I could see he wasn't all that different from me. Maybe, in another world, I'd have become a preacher.

"Actually I was hoping to meet you," he said.

"Yeah, why?"

"May's told me you take pictures for the newspaper."

"Yeah?"

He turned quiet, then began reluctantly. "Perhaps I shouldn't ask, but we wondered if you'd consider taking some photos at the food bank, and then get them in the paper. The publicity might help bring in donations. It's hard to keep going."

"No big corporate givers?"

"You're kidding." He laughed. "It's as hand-to-mouth as the people it serves."

"I'd certainly be willing to come by with my camera, but I can't promise anything for the paper. I'm just a stringer. Metling's the big man, and he and I run hot and cold. At the moment, it's pretty chilly," I said, remembering how I'd handled the pictures of the fire on Friday. "He has very clear ideas about what's appropriate news coverage, particularly with an election only a couple of weeks away. He may not want to make the economy look too bad."

"All I'm asking you to do is try," said Ruffing.

"Okay. I'll stop in this week."

"Thursday," he said, reaching for another sandwich.

"Thursday then."

"Somebody wants to see you upstairs," said Tattoo, suddenly standing in front of us.

"I hope she's pretty," I answered.

But he didn't smile. Even in the bright electric light of his kitchen, amidst the chatter of the wake, his face was as serious as it had been in the glow of the flames from the burning house.

"It's a cop," he said.

··· 12 ···

"You Jack Reese?"

"Yeah."

"You're a photographer?"

"I try."

The cop flashed his badge. "You're the one who spotted the fire and reported a Volkswagen parked in the middle of Baxter Street that night?"

"One and the same."

He stood in Tattoo's doorway and peered into the living room. "Can we talk here, or is there a better place?"

"You want to go next door to my house?" I asked.

"This may take a while. There are people downstairs, aren't there?"

"We're holding a sort of wake for Daniel Jones."

"I'm sorry I interrupted," he said. But he made no offer to come back another time.

"Okay, let's go over to my place," I finally said.

I opened the door and led him across the short length of sidewalk to my porch. He followed me silently, a slight swing to his arms. He had a large brown envelope in his hand. I wondered if he had a gun under his black quilted jacket. I finally guessed he did. Weren't all detectives supposed to?

I had no idea how many detectives were on the Shawnee police force, or how they stacked up against the tough plainclothes variety you saw in the movies, but the detective seemed formidable and intimidating enough to me. A child of the sixties, I could be put on edge easily by police, even when I had no reason to be.

His name was Edward Harter, and he looked to be about ten years older than me, in his early forties, though it was hard to tell from his expressionless face, a face that was starting to show lines of wear. His brown hair was shorter than mine but scruffy. He was solid enough that I wouldn't have wanted to chance finding out what kind of shape he was in. Maybe about six foot, my height, he was at least twenty-five pounds heavier.

Inside my front room, I switched on a light and motioned him to sit at the rickety desk chair. I went back to the studio and returned with the stool for myself. The moment I climbed on it, I was glad I had the high seat, looking down on him, not vice versa.

"This where you do your business?" he asked, taking in the room, from the peeling wallpaper to the pile of stuff on the table next to him.

"I use this room for an office and the back one for a studio."

He pulled a small notebook and pen from his jacket pocket. "How did you come to notice the fire?"

"I was up late and looked out the kitchen door and saw flames in the alley."

"Then you called the fire department?"

"No. I ran down to see if I could do anything. I yelled and yelled, hoping to wake people up. May, the woman next door, actually called in the fire, I think."

Harter nodded and jotted a few notes. "When you got to the alley, Baxter Street, you saw Daniel Jones' house burning, and you found a car parked in the middle of the street?"

"Right, the Volkswagen."

"Empty?"

"Yeah. I wasn't expecting it to be there. I rammed my knee into the back bumper and twisted my ankle. Turned out the keys were in it. Later I moved the thing after we decided it would be in the way of the fire trucks."

"We?"

"Tattoo and I. He's the one who answered next door when you knocked."

"The old guy with one arm?"

"Right."

"He's married to this, uh, May?"

"Yeah."

"So you got into the Volkswagen and moved it?"

"I drove it down the alley and parked it. Left the keys in it. It was still there yesterday, I think."

"You didn't notice any personal articles inside? Papers, clothing, a purse, anything?"

"No."

"Was that the only time you were in the car?"

"Yeah."

"You have no idea who the Volkswagen belonged to?"

"I don't remember seeing it before."

"You never saw Susan Maddox Devendall driving it?"

"Who?"

"Susan Maddox Devendall."

"I never heard of her."

"Never met her?"

"Not that I know of."

He lifted the brown envelope from the floor, opened the flap, and pulled out a pile of photographs. I recognized the top one even before he handed them to me. There she was . . . in her little-girl costume, her legs kicking high, her white skirt flying, her thighs bare.

"Did you take those?" asked Harter, making no secret of how closely he was watching my eyes.

I flipped through the prints, studying them. I turned one over and read my name and address stamped on the back.

"Yeah. Is she this. . . ?"

"Susan Maddox Devendall. Her mother-in-law found those pictures at her home."

"I didn't even know her name. The car was hers?"

He nodded, then asked, "You took her picture and didn't know who she was?"

"That's not unusual, is it?"

"You tell me, you're the photographer."

"She came on Monday and asked me to photograph her and came back the next day for the prints. She paid in cash. What's the big deal?"

"She seems to have disappeared after she left her car behind your house on the night of the fire. Her body was discovered last night."

"Her body?"

I began to understand his visit. I glanced down at the photos in my hand and realized the position I was in. She'd disappeared and turned up dead after I'd taken some questionable photos of her. She'd turned up missing the same night as the fire down the hill from me—a fire I'd been the first to notice.

He reached over and took back the pictures. "Were these all taken on Monday then?" he asked.

"No. The ones of just her head are from Monday. She said she needed a passport photo by the next day. When she came back on Tuesday, she asked me to take the others. She was wearing that costume. She picked them up on Wednesday."

Wednesday. Christ. I remembered Wednesday's session all too well. Her in "her mother's" pink dress, stripping down.

Harter was staring at my face and eyes. I forced myself not to look toward my desk, where, amid the other clutter, the photos from Wednesday were. It was better not to tell him, unless he asked.

"Wednesday was the last time you saw her?"

"Yeah, but . . ."

"But what?"

"She called me up Thursday night."

"The night of the fire?"

"Yeah."

"What'd she want?"

"To come over and have more pictures taken." And, I failed to add, to pick up Wednesday's lingerie shots.

"When did she call?"

"Around midnight."

"She called you up at midnight and asked to come over?"

"Yeah. She'd apparently been here earlier in the evening but I was out."

"Where were you?"

"I was at Reverend Richard Baum's church taking a picture of some preachers giving Congressman Canley an award."

"Preachers and a congressman?" he asked, glancing at her legs as he slid the prints back into the brown envelope.

"I work sometimes for *The News*."

"I thought maybe you took pictures for *Playboy* or something."

I didn't like the remark. His next question was worse.

"Did you ever sleep with this woman?"

"What kind of question's that?" I asked, surer than ever that I'd volunteer nothing about Wednesday evening.

"A logical question," said Harter. "A married woman comes to have pictures like these taken, then later calls you up at midnight and wants to come over—and ends up murdered."

"No, I didn't sleep with her. I didn't know she was married. I didn't even know her name. I don't know how she was killed or where you found her body, either."

"So she just calls up and asks if she can come over?"

"Right."

"What happened then?"

"I made coffee and waited for about an hour. I happened to look out the kitchen door and see the fire. I ran down to see what was going on and ran into the Volkswagen. I moved the car so the fire trucks could get to Daniel's house."

I wondered if I sounded as irritated as I felt. If I did, Harter didn't care. He continued with his questions.

"Did you know Daniel Jones well?"

"Fairly well. I grew up in this neighborhood. I've talked to him a few times in the last couple of months."

"Anything strike you as particularly odd about the fire?"

"How do I answer that? The fire struck me as particularly odd. I don't normally see old men get burned alive. I guess the oddest thing was the car. I told the fire marshal and the police about the car that night. Everyone knew I moved it. Didn't you guys check into it?"

"Everyone didn't know you knew the woman it belonged to," responded Harter.

"I didn't know it was hers."

"You didn't see any sign of Mrs. Devendall or anyone else?"

"No."

"You wonder why she didn't show up?"

"Yeah, but what was I supposed to do? Call the police and say a mystery woman didn't come for a middle-of-the-night photo session? I figured she saw the fire and all the activity and decided to go home. I haven't heard from her since."

"Did you expect to?"

"I guess I did. Like you keep pointing out, she called me at midnight."

"You're telling me you never saw her that night and you didn't know it was her car and you were never in the vehicle except to move it for the fire engines?"

"That's what I keep telling you over and over. It's the truth."

"You never saw that car during any of her other visits?"

"I didn't know how she got here."

"You have no idea why she vacated her vehicle on the night of the fire?"

"None at all."

"Do you think she knew Daniel Jones?"

"I certainly never saw them together or heard them mention each other."

"Do you spend a lot of time in the alley?"

"I don't know what you're after. My backyard faces on the alley. My car's back there. We all use it as a shortcut down the hill. Sometimes I go out back in the evening. Sometimes I visit Daniel."

Harter flipped back through his notebook as if he were looking for something. Finally, he found it. "You were out in the alley last Wednesday night, weren't you?"

"Yeah. How do you know that?"

"An officer on patrol remembered seeing someone behind your house."

"Can't I be out in my own backyard?"

"What were you doing?"

"Thinking. What do you do in your backyard?"

"Was this before or after she stopped by for these photographs?"

"After. She left fairly early. I remember the police car going by about ten. I'd already been outside a while."

"You hadn't noticed anything unusual going on around Daniel Jones' house lately?"

"No."

"No strangers or vehicles?"

"Nothing I recall."

"He didn't have any enemies, did he?"

"He was almost eighty-five years old," I said.

"That's not what I asked."

"I imagine Daniel had outlived most of his enemies. I don't know anyone who hated him."

"Is there anything else?"

"What?"

"Anything else you should tell me?"

I ran the events of Wednesday night through my head again, then answered, "No."

The detective closed his notebook. "What was she like, this Susan Maddox Devendall?"

"When she was here, she was rather nervous. Reluctant at first to relax for the camera. She said that's why she wanted those photos taken in costume. She was, maybe, sort of disconnected a bit."

When I didn't offer more, he rose from the chair.

"What happened to her? How did she die?" I asked before he could leave.

"I guess you'll be reading about it in the paper tomorrow anyway," he said, his voice a little softer than it had been. "She apparently left home late Thursday night or early Friday morning, and then it's all a blank until her body was found last night in the canal. She'd been beaten. She was wearing only jewelry. A raincoat and a lot of jewelry."

"You think her death and Daniel's are related somehow?"

"I'd say I have to think so, at least right now."

"Am I a suspect then?"

"Let's just say you're the only one who knew both victims."
He stepped toward me and pulled a card out of his pocket.
"Here, if you think of anything else, call me."

For a long while after he'd gone, I sat on the stool and fingered his card.

Had he known I hadn't told him everything? Had I given myself away?

I hadn't lied. I'd answered his questions. He hadn't asked about Wednesday night's session. What good would it have done to have shown him those photos? They would only have dirtied her reputation more. And mine.

Found dead in only her jewelry and raincoat. So that was Thursday's child.

I glanced at the envelope that contained Wednesday's prints. I could destroy them, burn them, cut the negatives in fragments and dump them in the trash.

But what if they truly mattered? What if they had something to do with why she'd been murdered?

How could they? I was innocent, whatever Harter believed. And what could those photos, what could she, have had to do with Daniel?

"You're the only one who knew both victims," he'd said.

As if to put me on notice.

He didn't have to tell me.

I was a suspect all right.

My head suddenly felt like someone had cracked it with an ax.

··· 13 ···

The dream came for the first time Sunday night.

I was asleep in the top floor of a very old, very tall, narrow, four-story, paint-bare frame house.

I was awakened by the noise of a burglar somewhere downstairs.

So what do you do?

You brave it.

You climb out of bed and go in search of him.

You run down to the third floor, where you see a dry old wooden table with a tall thin candle on it and the candle falls over before your eyes and immediately the table starts to burn like paper and you run over and try to smother the flames with your bare hands.

Then you run down to the second floor of the dry-as-kindling house and see a dry old wooden table with a tall candle on it and the candle falls over before your eyes and the table starts to burn like paper and I run over and try to smother the flames with my bare hands.

Then you run down to the bottom floor of the old house and see a dry wooden table with a tall candle on it and the candle falls over before my eyes and the table starts to burn like paper and I run over and try to smother the flames with your bare hands.

Upstairs there is the noise of a burglar somewhere.

So I run up to the second floor of the house and see a wood table with a tall candle on it and the candle falls and the table starts to burn like paper and you run over and try to smother the flames with my bare hands.

Then you run up to the third floor and see a table with a tall candle and the candle falls and the table starts to burn and I run over and try to smother the flames with bare hands.

Then I run up to the top floor and a table with a candle and candle falls and table starts to burn and I run over try to smother flames with bare hands.

Downstairs there is the noise of a burglar.

...

EDWARD HARTER

...

··· 14 ···

Sometimes they simply lied.

Sometimes they didn't lie but they weren't forthcoming with the truth, either.

Sometimes the truth was hard to take.

Harter didn't know which category the photographer belonged in.

Monday morning at his desk, he remained unsatisfied with his first questioning on the case. Jack Reese's story was so scattershot the unnamed woman who had posed suggestively and called him at midnight on the night of the fire and left her car behind his house and ended up dead in the canal—so scattershot that it was hard to see the target.

Susan Devendall or Daniel Jones? Which case was he working on?

The way he saw it, finding an opening in the old man's killing was a tougher proposition than finding someone to talk to about Susan Maddox Devendall. At least she had had a husband and, presumably, friends who might be able to explain her behavior.

Harter didn't know how other detectives worked. He'd spent his career as one of only two full-time investigators on the Shawnee police force. He'd pretty much taught himself. Usually he began with the closest brick when building a case. Then he reached out a little farther for the next one.

Harter moved the papers around on his desk, wondering what bricks Reese was hiding. More and more, being a cop meant moving papers. He put one batch in a desk drawer. He tossed another on Caruthers' desk. Let him move them. Caruthers wouldn't complain much. He'd already been warned by the chief that he'd be picking up a lot of little stuff.

Caruthers didn't hate the paperwork as much as Harter. A day spent at his desk filling out reports and forms was just one less day Caruthers had to be on the street, one more day on the conveyor belt to retirement. Not that Caruthers was such a bad guy, or a bad cop. He was just tired.

Harter wondered if the chief would have given him such a free hand if there wasn't a Devendall body involved.

Maybe so.

Two killings in two days threw off all the crime stats for Shawnee. Like most blue-collar cities in the Alleghenies, Shawnee usually had a low incidence of violent crimes on the annual FBI reports. The big-city people had it wrong. The working-class mountain towns weren't really so rough and rowdy, though Shawnee could get rough and rowdy enough for him.

What Harter had originally planned for Monday was a visit to the Devendall family. To meet the husband. To talk to the mother-in-law who had reported the victim missing, the mother-in-law who had found the strange photographs. But they had put him off.

Howard Devendall had called first thing to say he had only returned to Shawnee late Sunday and would be busy with family matters all day, planning his wife's cremation and setting up the details of the memorial service set for Saturday, October 23.

Devendall added that his mother was very upset and it would be best to delay speaking to her, too.

So the interview had been set for Tuesday morning. All Harter could do in the meantime was work around the edges.

He read every shred of paper about the case—the fire marshal's report, the coroner's preliminary findings, the obituaries and articles in the newspaper, even notes on the kids who'd found the body—and he was bothered by the Volkswagen. Someone had screwed up by not seriously checking into it right off. There had been a note saying who it belonged to. That was all. Probably because the weekend had come, he told himself.

He kept returning to Jack Reese, the only apparent connection between the Devendall woman and the old railroader. He reminded himself to lay off the photographer for a couple of days. A watched pot never boils, his tea-drinking grandmother had always professed. So he'd let Reese simmer some before trying to pry the lid off the pot. He'd return to the house on Thomas Street in mid-week.

Hating the waiting, he hurried out of the office and headed to Baxter Street for another look at what was left of the Jones house.

No one was in the alley when he pulled his unmarked car off to the side and killed the engine. Climbing out, he glanced at the back of Reese's house, noting the window in the kitchen door from where Reese had said he'd seen the fire. Then he lit a cigarette and studied the ruin of the burned house. The charred fragments still glistened with moisture.

Thursday night, the old man had apparently been sitting in an overstuffed chair in the living room, right off the alley, when whoever came in came in. At least, that was the conjecture Harter had inherited from the fire marshal and the coroner. There was nothing left of the house or the overstuffed chair, and there'd been little left of the old man. Sometimes Harter wondered how such theories evolved, how anyone could be sure of anything.

Jones was believed to have been beaten and was probably unconscious or already dead when the place was doused with kerosene.

Susan Devendall had been beaten, too.

Harter dropped his cigarette into one of the puddles in the alley and it sizzled before it was soaked. Sunday night, for the third straight night, it had rained. The heavy downpour early Saturday morning had probably created the shallow pool in the canal where Susan Devendall's body had been dumped.

Dumped.

The coroner believed she'd been killed early Saturday and dropped facedown in the water.

Which meant she'd been somewhere for over twenty-four hours after abandoning her car in the alley.

Somewhere she'd stayed—or been kept—wearing only a raincoat and a barrelful of jewelry.

In all her gold and diamonds, she'd been on her way to a photographer in the middle of the night. Figure that out. His instinct told him Reese was holding back. But what—and why?

The coroner had detected no sign of recent sexual intercourse, rape or otherwise. So, neither sex nor robbery was the apparent motive.

"Ain't you solved it yet?"

Harter turned to see Reese's one-armed neighbor standing a few feet from him in the alley.

"Tattoo, isn't it?"

"How'd you know?"

"Jack Reese told me last night."

"Name's really Henry Kendall. They call me Tattoo. You know, you got Jack upset. He didn't have nothing to do with it."

"Why are you so sure?" asked Harter, watching the older man closely.

"I know him. Knowed him since he was a kid. If you'd seen him the night of the fire, seen how frantic he was about not being able to help Daniel, you wouldn't doubt it."

"You've got to understand. I'm supposed to doubt everything, to check out everything."

"So what do you think?"

"I don't know. It's too early. You knew Daniel Jones well, I take it."

"Yeah, 'course."

"You work with him on the railroad?"

"We both worked for the railroad, but we never worked together. He worked in the shops with Jack's grandfather. I was usually out on trains as a brakeman or something, till I lost my arm."

"Any reason anyone would want to kill him or burn his house down?"

"I got none. I don't figure he had buried treasure in the place. He was too harmless to hate."

"No family, huh?"

"None anyone knows of."

"He didn't tell you of anybody visiting lately? You didn't notice anybody prowling around, did you?"

"No."

"How about the Volkswagen in the alley that night—had you ever seen it before?"

"I don't think. I don't usually keep track of the traffic around here."

"Jack Reese moved the car that night?"

"Yeah. I told him to so's the fire trucks could get down the alley."

"When did you first notice the fire?"

"May and me was in bed and heard Jack yelling outside. I got dressed and run down while she called the fire department."

"What was Reese doing when you got here?"

"Staring at the flames, trying to decide whether to go in and try to pull Daniel out. I told him there was no use."

"You didn't spot a woman around, did you?"

Harter watched as Tattoo nervously shifted his weight from one foot to the other.

"You mean the one that went with the car?"

"Yeah, that's who I mean," said the detective.

"Only thing I know about her is a day or so before, Jack told me he was expecting some woman to come pick up a passport picture he'd taken."

"He never mentioned taking other pictures of her?"

"No. He never mentioned her any other way."

"Has he been busy with his photography lately?"

"Not that many paying jobs. A few for the newspaper. We went out the other morning to a train wreck."

"I saw it in the paper."

"He's been spending a lot of time taking pictures around town since he come back."

"When did he come back to Shawnee?"

"In early August. His tenant moved and he'd lost his job, so he come here for a while."

"How long had he been away?"

"Maybe fifteen years."

"What'd he do all that time?"

"I don't know much about it. I think he worked for a magazine. I told you, you're wasting your time checking on him. He's a good boy. Like everyone else, I'm sure you can find out things about him that he'd rather you didn't know, but he ain't no killer."

"I hope you're right," said Harter as he glanced again at Reese's tall, narrow brick house. "Look, I may come back and see you in the next few days. If you think of anything odd about last week, or anything I should know about Daniel Jones, call me."

He pulled a card out of his jacket and handed it to Tattoo. Then he climbed back in his car and headed down the alley and out onto the Avenue toward South Shawnee, past the railroad yards, toward the old Shawnee & Chesapeake Canal.

He'd only seen the spot where her body had been found in the cloudy dark of Saturday night. He'd been in the midst of a candlelight dinner at Liz's when the chief had called. They always knew where they could get him. And he always responded, even if it meant leaving a birthday meal.

He maneuvered through the cramped streets of Shantytown—or what had once been Shantytown but was now giving way to the prefab houses of a neighborhood they'd started calling Riverview. The collapsing canaller joints and shacks were, street by street, being ripped down and replaced with $60,000 aluminum-sided residences. The Shawnee city fathers and Chamber of Commerce were working on plans to turn the old canal itself into a public park. "The perfect hiking/biking trail," their brochure proclaimed. No one was anxious to save the canallers' shanties and haunts for posterity. They were too gritty for a park. They were eyesores.

He lit a cigarette as he turned onto the road that led to the arched bridge across the canal and over to the box factory. Just before he reached the bridge, he pulled off the road and parked behind a rusting Ford. He sensed immediately who it belonged to.

"You come here often?" Harter asked Jack Reese when they met on the towpath a few minutes later.

Reese, his camera hanging by a worn leather strap from his shoulder, was staring into a puddle of rainwater trapped in the abandoned canal.

"I wanted to see it. I read the morning paper and came out here." His voice betrayed an unmistakable nervousness.

"Well, this isn't the place," said Harter. He began to head down the towpath with long, quick strides. Reese fell in step alongside him.

"You been out here before taking pictures?" asked Harter. "I would think this place'd be a photographer's field day, what with all the locks and antique structures and stone walls and things."

"I haven't been here in years," answered Reese. "Not since I was a kid. After my grandfather retired from the railroad, he walked a lot for his heart. We'd come here and he'd tell me about the mule drivers and the flatboats and the winos sleeping under the bridges. He knew some people who lived in Shantytown, and we'd visit them."

"Yeah, they stayed around for years after the canal shut down, didn't they? Couldn't tear themselves away from this place. Home is home, I guess." Harter came to a stop. "Right over there's where the kids found the body."

He pointed across the canal to a small pond near a lock on the other side. Water had collected on a stone slab that was lower than the rest of the trench. The bank down to the pool was pockmarked with footprints and signs of Saturday-night activity. The kids, and later the police themselves, had mangled the muddy bank, so there was no chance of finding footprints.

"Did she drown there?" asked Reese.

"No, she was dead when she was put there. Multiple blows. The one to the head was the big one."

Harter looked sideways to size up Reese's reaction. Tattoo had claimed the photographer wasn't a killer, but there was no way to know. Harter believed almost anyone was capable of murder once they got started. Adrenaline could make up for size and initial lack of resolve. A baseball bat could make up for soft hands—especially when one victim was eighty-five years old and the other was a slim, manicured, unmuscled woman.

"Then they had to carry the body up the towpath quite a ways," said Reese, staring at the dirty water.

"Not necessarily. Look over at the other side. That's the parking lot for the box factory over there. They could have almost driven to the edge of the canal. If it was still dark, no one would have seen them."

"The cardboard box factory is closed down?"

"It's been gone since the late sixties."

"I didn't know. I was out of town then. Everything in Shawnee seems to be closing. What happened?"

"I don't know," said Harter after a minute's pause. "I'm a cop, not an industrialist. The workers there tried to start a union and the company moved away."

"Just like the steelworkers say Shawnee Steel is planning to?"

"Yeah, just like that."

"Sometime the cheap labor'll wise up," said Reese. "They'll get tired of breaking their backs for low wages and the allure of the Sunbelt will wear off."

Harter said nothing. That was his policy: Keep your opinions to yourself. He'd already said too much. Eventually he turned away and began walking back to the cars. He barely noticed Reese had caught up with him until the younger man asked a question.

"Are you originally from Shawnee?"

"Yeah," said Harter, volunteering nothing more.

"How'd you get to be a detective?"

"I needed a job."

When they reached the parked cars, Harter lit a cigarette and got in his vehicle. He rolled down the window and said, "Don't forget to call me if you think of anything," before turning around and slowly pulling away.

In the rearview mirror, he watched as Reese slid the camera off his shoulder and began walking over the bridge, over the canal, toward the old box factory.

··· 15 ···

A bright sun reflected off the roof and white walls of the Devendall mansion Tuesday morning as Harter backed into a parking spot on the street out front.

"*Mansion* is an exaggeration," Liz would lecture him. "Your class consciousness is showing. It's a character flaw. Can't you outgrow it?"

Like she had outgrown hers. Somewhere along the line, her training and clientelle had erased any "class consciousness" she had—if she'd ever had any to begin with. His own training and clientelle had just heightened his. Obviously, it was a sign of his origins that he'd parked on the street rather than circle up the drive to the front door.

Maybe it was best he and Liz didn't live together, he told himself.

Mansion or not, they didn't build houses like the Devendalls' anymore. For starters, you couldn't afford to heat them unless you had a hell of a lot of money to begin with. And without servants, there weren't enough hours in the day to keep such a place up. You could spend the warm-weather days just keeping the garden in shape. You could spend your winters just clearing the snow off the walks and driveway.

Carrying a brown envelope, Harter walked up the brick path

past a Shawnee Historical Society plaque that proclaimed the house had been built in 1855 by one Shriver Devendall, a railroad and coal speculator who had been a state legislator before the Civil War.

A maid in a gray pinstriped dress answered his rap on the door with the knocker. Harter had seen the black maid and the spacious entry hall before.

Sunday afternoon, Amy Devendall had called headquarters to say she'd discovered something unusual in her daughter-in-law's room. When Harter had arrived, the maid had handed him a sealed envelope. Mrs. Devendall, she'd said, was in bed and didn't wish to see anyone. Howard Devendall hadn't yet returned to Shawnee.

Outside, in his car, Harter had torn open the envelope and found the photos. Jack Reese's name was stamped on the back of each one.

This time, the maid led him down the entry hall and into a large room that looked like an antique shop. Leatherbound books lined the walls. The massive Victorian furniture made it seem as if Shriver Devendall himself had just risen from his pigeonhole desk and left for a moment.

Mr. Devendall had gone to his office and would be back shortly, said the maid. Mrs. Devendall would be with him directly. Her tone of voice made it sound almost like a warning.

Harter sat down and felt even more out of place when he realized he was on a loveseat. Liz would have laughed at how he squirmed.

He placed the brown envelope on the plush material next to him and rested his hand on top of it. Through the paper he could feel the jewelry that had been taken from Susan Devendall's body.

After leaving Reese at the canal Monday, Harter had spent the afternoon showing off the necklace, bracelets, earrings, and various gold chains to Shawnee jewelers. Usually such rounds were the kind of thing he tried to pawn off on Caruthers or some beat cop, but, having nothing productive to do, he'd gone to the jewelers himself.

No one could identify a thing. Could be imported, one had said. Could be made by one of those hippies who sell at craft fairs, according to another. "Custom-made. We don't stock anything like this," a third had said, holding up the largest chain with obvious distaste.

"Detective Harter?" she said before he was aware she was in the room.

He rose from the loveseat. "Hello, Mrs. Devendall. I came to ask you a few questions."

"I know," she said in a manner that somehow translated into "You may." Crossing the red swirls of the Oriental carpet, she arranged herself carefully in a chair beside the elaborate desk.

Amy Devendall looked to be in her seventies, and well taken care of. She was dressed to the teeth, false or not, and looking at her Harter figured she always was. She carried the smell of perfume with her. She said nothing. Just waited for him to begin.

Finally he asked, "Do you have any idea what may have happened to your daughter-in-law?"

"No," she said, clearly and forthrightly.

"As I understand it, your son was out of town all week," said Harter, starting with the basics.

"Howard was in Pittsburgh on business for Shawnee Steel. As you may know, he is an attorney. He is on retainer with various industries to represent them in legal matters and government hoopla. He didn't feel like staying around the house this morning, so he went to his office. We expect him back at any moment, and you may ask him anything you like."

"Susan . . . your daughter-in-law didn't usually go on such business trips with him?"

"Rarely. After the first year or two of their marriage, she usually stayed home, especially if she was working."

"Working?"

"She was . . . I imagine you'd call her a social worker, if you can believe that."

"A social worker here in Shawnee?" asked Harter with some surprise. The obituary hadn't mentioned a job.

"Yes. What do they call it these days? The Department of Human Services? It's welfare no matter what they call it, isn't it? She worked for the welfare department on and off for years. Until this past summer. I always told Howard the girl felt guilty about being well off. She was rebelling against her father's wealth, and later against ours, if you ask me. It was all quite ridiculous. In the early seventies she went to anti-war demonstrations and all that. Howard fell head over heels for her when they met and was a long time in realizing how different they really were."

"When were they married?"

"Oh, I imagine it was 1977. Yes, it was a week or two after the peanut farmer became president."

"She was working for Human Services then?"

"I believe that was when she first quit for a time. Then she went back."

"And she quit again this summer? Was there a reason?"

"A very good reason. A colored man tried to rape her last spring. She was never the same afterwards."

"When was this?"

"I should think it was early April. She quit in August."

"Do you know the man's name?"

"No. I'm sure the welfare people could tell you. Do you believe it has something to do with her . . . her murder, Detective Harter?"

"It's hard to say. I'll check it out. Is there anything else you know about the attempted rape?"

"Howard wanted to prosecute the man, but Susan wouldn't let him. I believe she was afraid of what would happen when she went back to the colored neighborhood. For a time, they transferred her to a position working with old people, but she'd finally come to her senses. She didn't explain it to me, but I saw signs that she was suddenly interested in clothes and social functions—all the things she'd once made fun of. Susan, you must understand, did not confide in me. I'm not sure she confided in Howard, either."

"Who might she have confided in?"

Amy Devendall folded her hands in her lap. "She didn't have many women friends. Odd, isn't it, how these attractive modern girls come and go and pride themselves on freedom, yet make so few quality friends?"

"I wouldn't know," said Harter. "Am I to assume that your son and his wife weren't very close?"

"Ask Howard."

Put off by the chill in her voice, he changed course. "When was the last time you saw your daughter-in-law alive?"

"It would have been late Thursday evening. I thought I heard the television—the eleven o'clock news—in her room when I retired. She often stayed up watching the news or movies. Sometimes she left the house at night, especially when Howard was away, though I'm sure she didn't know I knew."

"You believe she was alone at the time you passed her door?"

"Certainly," said Amy Devendall, almost challenging his question.

"Was she home every evening last week?"

The response was a long time coming. "No."

"What night was she gone?"

"She left early Wednesday night and must have returned after

I was in bed. Tuesday evening she was also out. Howard called home that night and I was forced to tell him I didn't know where Susan was. I sensed he expected as much."

"You have no idea where she was those nights?"

"No. I frequently had no idea what she did."

"Did she always drive the Volkswagen?"

"Yes. Howard offered her a new sports car for running about town, but she preferred the Volkswagen. To hide her position, I believe. She didn't want her customers to smell her money."

"Her customers?"

"The welfare types."

"Her clients?"

"Yes."

"So you have no idea where she went Tuesday, Wednesday, or Thursday night?"

"I said I didn't."

"When did you decide to tell the police she was missing?"

"Saturday morning, after she'd been away two nights. Howard had called again on Friday evening to say he would have to stay in Pittsburgh longer than he'd planned. He asked about her and again I told him she wasn't home. I was worried, and on Saturday morning I called the police. I didn't know what else to do."

"She'd never stayed away that long before?"

"No," she said, biting off further explanation.

"She made no attempt to contact you or your son after Thursday evening?"

"We heard nothing until the officer came to the door Saturday night and said her body had been found in the canal. I immediately called Howard. Neither of us could begin to imagine what she'd been doing on that side of town."

"Where might you have expected her to be?"

"I certainly expected her to be at home, not out prowling the city," snapped Amy Devendall.

"Any idea who she might have been with on the nights she was out?" he pressed.

After a pause, Amy Devendall said, "I would only be guessing, and I prefer not to guess about such matters."

"Your guess could be the best lead I've got," he tried.

"Sorry, I can't help you. I'm in no position to know with certainty. Have you talked with that photographer?"

"He claims he didn't even know her name. Says she simply came and paid for some photos to be taken. Some of them may have been for a passport. Was she planning a trip?"

"Not to my knowledge."

"You found the pictures in her room Sunday?"

She nodded slowly. "I went in to look around. I was too upset to go to church. I was waiting for Howard to return home or call with word about when he would. I walked around the house, then looked in her room. I imagined I was doing the police a favor."

"Could I see Susan's room?"

"I'm sure you could force me to show you if I said no."

"Yes, I could."

"Then I suppose we better get it over and done with."

She rose from the desk chair and began walking from the room. Harter followed her back into the hallway and down to a staircase that spiraled upward. The way Amy Devendall gripped the bannister and slowly climbed the steps forced Harter to remember her age. No matter how good a job he wanted to do, no matter how much he disliked her, she *was* an old lady—an old lady who'd had to face up to the scandalous death of a daughter-in-law she obviously hadn't approved of.

Scandalous. Not a word he'd normally use. But one he figured Amy Devendall would.

Having navigated the stairway, she led him to a closed door. She pushed it open and stayed in the hall as she waved her hand for him to enter.

"Your son and his wife had separate bedrooms?" asked Harter as he scanned the light-filled room. Lace curtains covered the large windows, allowing the sunlight in. Between two of the windows was an antique canopied bed.

"Of course they each had their own room," said Amy Devendall, as if the thought of the two sharing a room—sharing a bed—had never occurred to her.

"Are most of Susan's things in this room?"

"I haven't removed anything but the photos," she said defensively.

"No, I meant she doesn't have another room for a study or anything?"

"Her things are here."

Harter crossed the lush ivory carpet and looked down at the combs, brushes, lipsticks, and makeups laid out on a vanity with a round full-length mirror.

"When you looked, did you notice whether anything was missing?"

"Taken?" she asked, misinterpreting him again.

"No. Had she packed a bag?"

Before answering, Amy Devendall came into the room and crossed to a white door. She opened it and stepped into a large walk-in closet. After some poking around, she said, "As far as I can judge, everything is here. I didn't even know she had so many clothes. I've never seen some of them. When she was a social worker, she always claimed she didn't care about clothes. She almost never wore makeup. Howard and I would have to convince her to spruce herself up. Some of these things are brand new." She reached forward, moved a pink dress, and looked down. "Her overnight case is here. We keep the luggage in the attic. I'll have Martha check if you like."

"I'd appreciate it," said Harter. "Just where did you find the photos Sunday morning?"

"In the dresser . . . in her lingerie drawer. I'll tell you, I was taken aback by some of the pictures."

"Did you find anything else odd?" asked Harter, crossing to the dresser.

"'Odd' is such an odd choice of words. Let's say, nothing else like the photographs."

Harter slid open a dresser drawer and glanced down at underwear, bras, slips in all styles and colors. "This where you found them?"

"Yes."

"You've looked through all the other drawers?"

"Yes."

He turned and stared at her. "There were no notes or love letters or good-bye messages or anything along those lines?"

"No," she answered, without half the offense he had feared. Maybe he was wearing her down.

He opened a jewelry box on top of the dresser. It was nearly empty.

"Susan didn't wear much jewelry," explained Amy Devendall before he could ask. "I think it was like the Volkswagen. Howard was always offering to buy her things, but she said no."

He closed the box. "What was she wearing when you last saw her?"

She reached inside the closet and held up the sleeve of a silk Oriental robe. "This is what she had on before she came up to her room. She bought it this summer."

"Do you know what she was wearing the other nights when she went out?"

"Not exactly. She wore a raincoat when she left the house. Just an old raincoat she'd had for years and wore to work."

"Mother!"

Mrs. Devendall stepped away from the closet and back out into the hall.

"We're upstairs, Howard," she called.

Harter stood next to the dresser and waited for his first glimpse of Susan's husband. For all intents and purposes, her *estranged* husband, it seemed. Having seen the young woman in Reese's photos, he wasn't prepared for Howard being as old as he was. Mid-forties at least. Maybe fifteen years older than his wife.

For a minute, he found it hard to concentrate on Howard's features. His face was so ashen and his eyes so pale that the man's head nearly blended into the light walls. His gray hair did little to destroy the illusion.

"This is Detective Harter, dear," Howard Devendall's mother told him. "He wanted to see Susan's room. I didn't think it would hurt."

"No, whatever the police want," said Devendall. The way his jaw clenched as he talked and his movements as he stepped into the room showed Harter that the pale lawyer did have some muscle attached to his rather boyish frame.

"I don't believe we've met before," said Harter. "I know most of the attorneys in Shawnee."

"I don't take criminal cases," Devendall said. Then, brusquely, he asked, "Is there anything else you'd like to see while you're here, Detective?"

"I don't think I have to see any other room in the house. But I'd like to talk to you, if I could."

"Shall we go back downstairs then?" asked Devendall.

"Fine."

The word was barely out of Harter's mouth before Amy Devendall was leading the way down the hall, then the stairs. He found himself feeling a little claustrophobic sandwiched in between her and her tall, pale son as they descended the curving staircase.

"We'll really have to paint the bannisters and the wooden trim this year, Howard," said the old woman, fingering the railing as she reached the bottom. "You wouldn't believe how much work is involved in simply preserving one's inheritance, Mr. Harter."

"Oh, I'd believe it."

"Families that don't take care of what they have are the ones who don't keep it for long," she continued. "Whether it's a house or a reputation, one must constantly work at it." She came to a stop at the library door. "You two go in and talk. I'll leave you alone. I could have Martha bring you some sandwiches for lunch, if you like."

"That would be good," said Devendall.

"And I won't forget, Detective Harter," she added before she disappeared into the house. "I'll have Martha go up to the attic and see that all the luggage is there."

Harter was sure Amy Devendall never forgot to attend to such details. He was almost as sure all the suitcases would be in their proper places.

Inside the library again, Harter picked up the evidence envelope from the loveseat. This time he staked out the desk chair for himself.

He waited for Howard Devendall to relax into a seat before opening the envelope and pouring the jewelry onto the desk.

"Do you have any idea where this came from?" he asked.

As with the luggage, he thought he knew what the answer was going to be.

··· 16 ···

After he left the Devendall mansion—he'd stick with that word—Harter spent a chunk of the afternoon making a stream-bank check.

He had a friend who worked for the State Health Department. Sometimes, when the guy had inspected enough septic systems and taken enough water samples and bagged enough rabid animals for the lab, he'd drive out into the mountains to make what he called a stream-bank check.

Which really meant he'd sit on a stream-bank and check the state of his mind. And body.

Harter's stream-bank checks rarely involved much real communing with nature. Sometimes he simply drove around Shawnee, the city he knew like the brown of his own eyes. Once in a while, he would drive south of town to the overlook on the mountain. From there he would stare down on the city where he'd been born and wonder what he was doing. Occasionally, he would show up at Liz's at lunchtime in hopes she was alone and had time to hold him.

This Tuesday, however, he merely drove long through the west side of town, past the big houses, some even bigger and grander than the Devendall period piece. When he tired of the west side, he headed east, crossed the river bridge, ducked through the underpass, and headed toward downtown Shawnee from the south.

Passing the idle Shawnee Steel mill he noticed that about a dozen men were still carrying signs on the cracked sidewalk outside the huge plant building. They probably had nothing else to do. Day after day, week after week, they would picket, their numbers slowly dwindling.

Harter had seen many pickets in his day. The bitterest times he personally remembered had been during the long rail strikes of the mid-1950s and late 1960s. Some of his own relatives had even been involved. He'd seen winter days when the men built fires in oil drums to warm their hands so they could keep going. They had acted like their lives were at stake, and he guessed they were.

He had had two uncles who didn't speak for fifty years because one of them had been a scab in the twenties. Better to starve to death than to cross a picket line, his father had always said.

He didn't know what he would do if he was ever called on to move against strikers. Maybe he'd sit down, resign, or be fired. Sometimes it was strange being a cop, representing the so-called law.

The steel mill might be closed, but the big shots hadn't stopped their activity. Lights burned in some of the offices. And Howard Devendall had been sent to Pittsburgh on company business the week before. He could have been making plans to move the mill south, like the pickets claimed, or to farm their jobs out to Korea or Taiwan. He'd told Harter he'd taken a charter flight on Sunday evening, October 10. Everything had been perfectly normal when he'd left Shawnee's small airport. Whatever *normal* meant.

From what he'd heard so far, Harter didn't consider Howard and Susan Devendall's marriage "perfectly normal." They had met at her father's funeral, Devendall had told him, after they'd gotten over the hump about the jewelry he couldn't identify. Oh, Howard had seen Susan at social events before, he'd said. He'd rather watched her grow up. But it was at Mr. Maddox's funeral in 1976 that they'd gravitated to each other. Susan, then twenty-three, was alone, her mother having died when she was fifteen.

She had been close to her mother, said her husband. Probably closer than she could ever be to anyone else again. Her mother had been a nurse who'd married the president of the hospital board of directors. Susan wanted to help people too, but she didn't have the patience for nursing. So she became a social worker. At the time of her father's death, at the time Howard and Susan began their courtship, she'd taken a long leave of absence and was unsure whether she'd return to work.

She went through those periods, Devendall said. Sometimes she enjoyed spending money, shopping, and living a life of leisure. Other times she felt the compulsion of a career.

No one had expected their marriage, least of all his mother, who had never liked Susan, or vice versa, he admitted. But Susan had wanted the company and a more settled life. He had wanted a wife, and had begun to believe he wanted a son.

Before long, Susan grew bored and went back to social work. There was to be no child. They comfortably went their own ways. Sometimes they didn't sleep together for months at a stretch.

Yes, she had changed in the last year. He couldn't put his finger on it. There had been the attempted rape in April, but the change had started before that. After the rape, she no longer had the nerve to visit the Negro projects. Her opinions had grown more conservative. She'd seemed less involved in her work. Ask her supervisor at the Department of Human Services, insisted Devendall, giving Harter a name and number.

So, Tuesday afternoon, after losing a few hours on his stream-bank check, Harter sat down at his desk, called the welfare office, and made an appointment with a Linda Dean for Wednesday morning.

Then he moved the "bricks" around on his desk again. Among them now was the report on the fingerprints found in the Volkswagen. Only two sets—the victim's and Jack Reese's.

"How's it going, Harter?" asked Caruthers when he came into the office they shared.

"Could be better," Harter answered, watching the medium-sized man collapse into his chair.

Harter always described Caruthers as "medium." Medium height. Medium weight. Medium-length salt-and-pepper hair. Medium voice. Medium viewpoints. Medium intelligence. If there was such a thing as the medium American, Caruthers was him, from the informality of his sportcoat to the practicality with which he approached problems.

"If you need any help on the case, checking anything out, let me know."

"There's nothing I can't handle yet," said Harter, playing his cards close.

"That won't make the chief's day."

"What are you on to?"

"A couple of B and E's, some vandalisms at vacant warehouses. They seemed related. Probably kids."

"You'd think they'd at least have the smarts to break in someplace with something worth stealing," said Harter, lighting a cigarette. Caruthers, like Liz, hated it when he smoked. Sometimes he smoked up the room just to drive the other detective out.

"You going to Liz's tonight?" asked Caruthers, flipping through the papers on his desk.

"No, you know the routine by now. Just Wednesdays and weekends. The other weeknights she has classes."

"So you'll head back to your lonely apartment and pop a TV dinner in the oven. You two really ought to get married."

"You forget I've been married, and I don't cook TV dinners," said Harter, blowing smoke toward Caruthers' desk. "I hate the mashed potatoes and peas and the little helpings. Tonight I'll feast. One of Mattioni's deluxe hoagies."

"You'll die eating that stuff."

"You tell me what could be healthier than a chef's salad on an Italian roll. Meatloaf?" He snubbed out his cigarette butt.

"I like meatloaf," said Caruthers.

"I don't," said Harter, putting on his black jacket and heading for the door.

Outside headquarters he turned right and quickly walked the two blocks to Mattioni's. Pushing open the heavy glass door, he breathed in that spicy salami-and-olive-oil aroma. Better than Amy Devendall's heavy perfume had been, that was for sure.

The evening line was shorter than at lunchtime, when a dozen or more downtown workers, courthouse employees, street punks, and cops might crowd into the small place. Sometimes you could wait in that line forever.

No matter how long the line got, however, old man Mattioni kept the same pace and ignored all but the customer in front of him. One sandwich at a time. He even refused to cut a pile of thin salami ahead of time. Everything cut fresh every time, no dried edges, no brown lettuce, no waste. Mattioni had no desire to turn out less than a masterpiece. Amazingly, it was also one of the cheapest subs in town.

The old man, nearly always silent, nodded a good evening to Harter as he slid his cash across the counter. Harter picked up his hoagie, and went back to the street. At his car, he climbed in, and drove away from the downtown, across the tracks, and up the hill into East Shawnee.

He turned onto his narrow side street and slipped the stick into reverse after turning off the engine. Once inside the turn-of-the-century frame house, he climbed to the third floor.

The apartment was big enough for Harter's needs. A living room, simple, modern, angular. A kitchen, large enough to eat in but small enough to reach the tan refrigerator from anyplace in it. A bedroom, roomy enough for a king-sized bed, with a closet that more than held his clothes. A bathroom that worked.

He'd been glad to find the place in a rush eight years before. The living room even offered a view of the abandoned Shawnee–Potomac passenger station. He hoped they wouldn't replace it with a Holiday Inn, like the plans called for.

He put the hoagie down on the low wooden table in front of the couch, took off his jacket and gun, and went to the kitchen for a Coke. Then he switched on the evening news.

Shawnee didn't have a television station, but the Bartlesburg station, fifty miles to the east, came in on cable, and WBRT made at least a cursory attempt to cover Shawnee. It was a "Good News" station, custom-made for the eighties, given to footage of Rotary clubs, visiting congressmen, charity bazaars, fashion shows, boy scouts, and the like. For the most part, WBRT didn't cover Shawnee's crimes. So far the only reports he'd seen about Susan Devendall or Daniel Jones had been the simple facts in *The News*, and *The News* had had nothing new to say Tuesday morning. He hoped it stayed that way for a while. He was sure Amy Devendall, with her concern for her family's reputation, felt the same way.

The Devendalls must have hated even the limited publicity they'd gotten. It certainly had *National Enquirer* possibilities: NUDE, BEJEWELLED SOCIALITE FOUND IN SHANTYTOWN. Except that Susan Devendall might have fought being depicted as the socialite her mother-in-law wished she would be.

Amy Devendall had carefully measured her words. She'd insinuated more than she'd said. Harter had decided her message was: Susan was a social worker. Imagine that! She'd spent her days with the shiftless. No wonder she had nearly been raped in the projects. No wonder she'd ended up in Shantytown. She shouldn't have been there.

Shantytown. When Harter had joined the force in the mid-sixties, there'd still been an aged cop or two around to fill him up with tales of Shantytown Saturday nights, when the hootch was blinding and the gambling fixed and the women lewd. They'd told him of heads crashed in by thick brown bottles and of bloated bodies floating until struck by passing canal boats.

He'd never expected to have his own tale, his own bashed-in head, his own body in the ditch. *And a west-side body at that.*

"You really should get over this class-conscious thing, this feeling you're working-class and the west-side people are the bosses and never the twain shall meet," Liz kept telling him.

Harter swallowed his last bite of hoagie, crumpled up the white butcher paper it had come in, and took the wad to the kitchen garbage can. Back in the living room, he turned off the TV and sprawled on the couch.

He wished he could see Liz right then. He'd joked about enrolling in one of her aerobics classes so he could see her more often. In the last couple of years, she'd been busier with exercise classes than with dance classes, a trend she didn't particularly care for. But she had to pay the bills, just like everyone else.

He grabbed the paperback book off the coffee table and opened it to his place. Liz was the one who'd suggested he give up Dashiell Hammett for Sinclair Lewis, a better writer than he'd expected. She'd been high on *Main Street*, with its careful piling up of facts about a small town, like clues in a mystery that never happened.

But he could only concentrate in spurts. When he'd reached his limit, he leaned his head against the arm of the couch and tilted it back so he was staring up at the Edward Hopper print on the wall. Liz had given him the street-corner scene two years before, after he'd been drawn to it in a museum shop during a weekend spent in New York. The brightly lit eatery in the black city night was like somewhere he'd walked into and out of many times. It could never pass as sheer decoration.

He lit another cigarette and let his thoughts drift back to a conversation they had once had.

"Maybe I shouldn't see things like I do, but I can't help it," he had said.

"With a little effort, you could help it," she'd responded.

"I keep thinking of John L. Lewis."

"Your family were railroaders, not coalminers. What do you know about John L. Lewis?"

"It's the idea. I've read that in the thirties—I don't know exactly when—John L. Lewis gave a speech about how the future belonged to the working people. He talked about the miners' children getting educations so they could become lawyers and teachers and doctors and help put the worker on equal footing with the bosses."

"So?"

"So it happened, and it didn't work. Millions of coalminers' kids and factory workers' kids and railroaders' kids have gotten more education. We became those lawyers, teachers, and doctors. We became artists, dancers, and detectives. We became middle-class. We stopped worrying about the people we came from."

"Stop feeling guilty," she'd said.

"I can't stop feeling it," he'd said. "All I can do is stop talking about it."

··· 17 ···

Harter took the orange plastic chair he was directed to and waited for Linda Dean.

He had no idea whether all days were so busy at the welfare office, but the place was certainly snapping Wednesday morning. There must have been a couple dozen people filling out forms or waiting for assistance in the Department of Human Services' downtown office. They made the storefront—an old shoe store that had been divided and subdivided into cubicles—seem crowded. Now and then a welfare worker would lead someone out of one of the cubicles and take another in.

Mostly the room was populated by women. The social workers were almost all women—at least the ones he could see. The people waiting were primarily younger women with screaming babies on their laps.

Deep down, Harter had his doubts about the welfare system, about whether it was possible to keep paying money to people who didn't work, who produced nothing but babies. He stared at the women, at the babies. It was beyond him what to do. Even if you put the kids in government day-care, it was no sure thing the mothers could find jobs these days. They looked so young, the mothers. He bet half of them had dropped out of high school pregnant.

The baby next to him was crying so loudly he didn't hear his name when the woman called it.

"Detective Harter?" she asked again, planting herself right in front of him. "I'm Linda Dean. Come this way."

He got up and followed her through the maze of cubicles until she ducked through a doorway and sat down behind a metal government desk that took up half her office.

"Like I told you on the phone, I'm looking for information about Susan Maddox Devendall," he said, sitting down.

"I was shocked when I read about it," said Linda Dean. "I don't know how Susan would have gotten herself into that situation."

"What situation?"

"I mean being found murdered in the canal."

"So I suppose you've got no thoughts on why she might have been in that area?"

"None at all."

"What was Mrs. Devendall like?"

Linda Dean nervously brushed back strands of her graying hair. "That's hard to say. I knew her for so long. I've been a supervisor for over ten years. I was the one who interviewed her for a job originally. She was fresh from college and had a definite social consciousness. I saw her moods over the years. It's hard to pinpoint the times when her personality changed drastically. I remember when she quit for a while, about the time her father died."

"Mr. Maddox died in 1976?"

"Yes. He'd been ill for months. We'd all been overworked here. The 1974–75 recession had strained us just like this one is doing. She said she 'wanted to take care of father in his last illness.' I thought she just wanted a break. I'd always been under the impression she and her father weren't very close."

"Her mother-in-law seems to think Susan Devendall was embarrassed about her family's wealth."

"Amy Devendall would think that."

"You know Amy Devendall?"

"Not very well. She isn't a fan of the Department of Human Services. From the way Susan talked about her, she wasn't a fan of Susan's, either. I shouldn't have said that. Mrs. Devendall could be right. Susan could have been rebelling against her family. Girls in their teens and early twenties do that, you know. Then, as they grow older, they often revert to the mores they grew up with. I'm sounding clinical, aren't I? Of course, her rebellious streak wouldn't have prepared anyone for her marriage to Howard Devendall."

"He was quite a bit older, wasn't he?" asked Harter.

"Yes." She seemed to calculate her words. "To be honest, I always believed she was seeking a father figure after Mr. Maddox died."

"She came back to work after her marriage?"

Linda Dean nodded. "Late in 1977, I think. I could get the exact date from her personnel file."

"I don't think that's necessary. Did you notice any change in her when she came back?"

Linda Dean considered what she was about to say. "She was still a good worker, though I believe the job wasn't as important to her. I was never quite sure why she stayed with it. The pay, of course, meant nothing. Twice I had to call her to ask her to cash her checks because the auditor was going crazy. She seemed more and more to have a split personality about her background and her job. She might have been guilty about her wealth, but she certainly wouldn't have wanted to be anything but rich. I know she'd been buying a lot of clothes, though she almost always wore an old skirt or jeans to work. She drove a

Volkswagen, but it was well-equipped, a stereo system and air conditioning. You figure it out."

"I'm told she changed even more after an attempted rape on the job."

"Yes."

"A black man?"

She nodded. "Susan was visiting clients in the public housing project and apparently became involved in a conversation with the man. She came back to the office very upset and claimed he'd tried to assault her. But she didn't press charges."

"Do you know who the man was?"

"Ace Stewart. That's a nickname, of course. I'm not sure of his real first name. I could probably look it up."

"James," said Harter.

"You know him?"

"Yeah."

"Is he a bad one? Could he have something to do with her death?"

Harter didn't answer. Instead, he asked, "She went on working?"

Looking a little irritated that he'd changed the subject, Linda Dean said, "She took a couple of weeks off. After she returned, she didn't want to go to the projects again, which I suppose would be a natural reaction. She asked what other jobs were available. I found her a position as an outreach worker with the Commission on Aging."

"When did she start with them?"

"Early in May. I believe she quit altogether at the beginning of August."

"Didn't like the job?"

"You'd have to talk to them. From what I hear, they were glad she quit. Here, see this woman," she said, scribbling a name and address on a slip of paper and sliding it over to Harter. "I could call her if you want and tell her you're coming."

"That would be good."

"Shall I say you're on your way?"

"I probably won't get there until afternoon," said Harter, stuffing the paper in the pocket of his jacket as he stood up. He'd decided to drop in on Ace Stewart and had no idea how long it would take.

As he drove, he wondered what kind of reception Ace would give him once the point of his visit became clear.

He'd known Ace Stewart most of his life. They'd grown up playing ball together in a burned-out lot on the fringe of what, in the 1950s, had been called the "colored" neighborhood. Amy Devendall still used the word colored. At least that was better than nigger.

When Harter was a kid, before the schools had been desegregated, before the blocks of row houses had been demolished in the name of urban renewal, before the projects had been built, Dab's Chicken House, long gone, had been the dividing line. The restaurant, with its reputed bookie joint in the rear, had stood on the corner of Grant and Lincoln, open to both races.

The brick row houses on the north side of the street hadn't seemed much different from the ones on the south. Maybe they were a little more run-down, but the only striking difference was that white railroad families, like Harter's, lived south of Dab's, while on the north side of the street most of the bodies were black.

Ace's father, a stooped but dignified man, had been a porter back in the days when porters and cooks were about the only Shawnee–Potomac jobs allowed to "coloreds"—Negroes—blacks.

When he had died in 1979, Harter went to the funeral and

then to the wake at the project apartment where Mrs. Stewart lived with her youngest daughter and her daughter's two children. Ace had just broken up with his wife at the time. There'd been something so melancholy about him that Harter could hardly stand it. He sensed the melancholy wasn't just Ace grieving for his father or singing the blues over his wife. It ran all the way through him.

Two years older than Harter, Ace had been the first black star of East Shawnee High's football team. That had been in 1957–58. Everyone expected he'd land a big scholarship and eventually make the pros. Somehow he hadn't. He'd gone to work for State Roads and, after the politics changed, managed to catch on with Shawnee Steel in the late sixties.

Harter dreaded what he was about to do. He didn't want to circulate through the projects looking for Ace or to knock on Mrs. Stewart's door asking about him. He didn't want to think about Ace Stewart almost raping Susan Devendall.

He turned the corner where the old black church had once been, and where he had often stood on Sunday nights to hear the rocking gospel music coming from inside. He'd never been able to relate to the neighborhood in the same way after they'd torn down the row houses and the church and put up the government housing. He wasn't convinced the projects were better than the way of life they'd replaced.

He got one break. As he'd hoped, Ace Stewart, too big for walls to hold in on a sunny day, was leaning on the mailbox in front of the projects.

Harter pulled up to the curb, reached across the seat to open the door, and said, "Climb in, Ace. Let's go for a ride."

They'd driven a block before Ace broke the silence. "We going to Jamaica?"

"I've got to ask you some questions," said Harter, glancing across the seat at the bulk of his old friend. Ace Stewart had upper arms like a woman's thighs. You had to study his face closely to notice his mustache and goatee.

"What about?"

"Susan Devendall."

"I didn't do nothing."

"I didn't say you did."

"She's got herself killed now."

"Yeah," mumbled Harter, pondering the way Ace had put it. "Let's start with last April."

"Refresh my mind."

"She claimed you tried to rape her."

"She come on to me. Don't you think I can tell when some woman comes up and's ready to rub herself all over you if you give her a shove?"

"And you gave her a shove?"

"I touched her arm. Honest, Harter, that's all I did."

"How'd you get in that situation with her in the first place?"

"You want the long or short version?"

"Try medium."

"This Devendall woman was visiting my sister for the welfare office. I'm living at home now that I'm single and laid off. So she's there and I come in and after a while my sister goes out to check on a kid or something. Mom wasn't around. So this woman asks what I'm doing home in the middle of the day and I tell her I got laid off before Thanksgiving, in the first batch of steel layoffs. After fourteen years—you believe that? So she says, You ain't been working for five months? I say, No. And she says, We gotta find you a job. And I say, Find one, I tried. She says they're hiring dishwashers at Maxi's and how someplace else needs a custodian and how I could go back to school for computer training. So I say, Look, lady, I'm a steelworker. I ain't no janitor or no busboy and I ain't good at books. She didn't like my answer much."

Ace stopped. Waiting for him to start again, Harter pulled a cigarette pack out of his black jacket and wiggled one free. "Smoke?"

Ace took the pack and pushed in the dashboard lighter. "You ain't gonna believe the rest of this, Harter. I don't know why I'm telling you."

"You're telling me 'cause I asked."

"She looks me over and says, I can see you're a steelworker. You're big and strong. And I say, Bet your ass I'm big and strong. She steps closer to me and has this look like she wants it, so I reach out and touch her arm."

"And?"

"And she screams her fucking head off, that's what she does. She screams and I back off and say I didn't do nothing to hurt her but by then she's running out the door and my sister's coming back in the room to see what's wrong."

"Nothing more?"

"Nothing more."

"Why'd you think she wanted it?"

"Come on, Harter. You can tell when a woman's on the make. You ever see me treat a woman wrong?"

"It doesn't jibe, Ace. Doesn't go with what we know about her."

"I didn't know nothing about her."

"She could have had anything she wanted. She had a rich lawyer husband and was wealthy herself. What would she have been messing with you for, and then screaming when you touched her?"

"Maybe she don't get along with her husband. Maybe it's like the old joke—she thinks she likes dark meat but when it's served up she gets scared. How the hell can I explain her? I told you you wouldn't believe it."

"You ever see her again?"

"No. Never saw her before and not again. A couple days after the thing, two guys come, say they're from welfare, and ask some questions. I keep waiting for something to come of it. You're the first one brought it up in six months."

"You don't know anything about her getting killed last week?"

"Just what the news says."

"Nothing out on the street about it?"

"Not a word."

Harter hit the brakes, backed the car up in an alley, and headed back to the projects, saying nothing.

"If I lie, cut off my dick," said Ace. "Ain't that what they used to do? Like robbers, they cut off their hands, and liars they cut out their tongues, and rapists they cut off their dicks. If I lie, cut out my tongue and cut off my dick. You think I want to live without talking and fucking?"

··· 18 ···

Sitting in his second social services office of the day, Harter just wanted to get the interview over with and go see Liz. Ace Stewart's words careened around his brain as if it were an echo chamber. They kept sounding long after he'd dropped Ace back at the mailbox, kept sounding as he'd driven crosstown to the Commission on Aging's Senior Center in an old elementary school, kept sounding as he sat across the desk from the Commission on Aging woman.

He couldn't keep her name straight. Good thing that Linda Dean had written it down for him. He'd forgotten it as soon as he'd asked for her. He kept looking at her green eyes and green eye makeup and green dress and thinking of her as Mrs. Green. Even her hair seemed tinged with green.

"I imagine Mrs. Dean told you the circumstances of how Susan Devendall came to work here for three months," she said.

He nodded. "What did she do here exactly?"

"She made home visits to see that senior citizens were all right and to sign people up for the hot-lunch program. I've pulled out a list of the folks she visited."

Harter took the neatly typed list and began scanning the names. Mrs. Green chattered on about office policy, how each outreach worker kept a log of her or his time, and then prepared a list of the people visited each week.

It sounded like all the red tape the police department bogged you down in, he thought.

Then he hit on the name.

"Daniel M. Jones," he read aloud.

Mrs. Green didn't react.

"You don't have a file on this Daniel M. Jones, do you?" asked Harter.

"Certainly."

She walked over to a wall of cabinets, opened a metal drawer and, without much fumbling, efficiently returned with a manila folder in her hand.

"Why are you so interested in him?" she asked, leafing through the folder before handing it over.

"He died in a fire last week, a suspected arson," answered Harter. "Susan Devendall's abandoned car was found nearby."

"I should have remembered that," said Mrs. Green, reaching for a paper from the file in front of him. "Susan visited Mr. Jones late in June. This is the application for hot lunches, and there should be some handwritten notes in there."

Harter found the yellow legal page with the notes. He was immediately disappointed. All Susan Devendall had written in her perfect round script was a sentence saying that Daniel Jones had been suggested as a meal client by a Reverend Ruffing and that she'd had to talk the old man into accepting free meals.

"Not much here," he said.

"The application just has information you probably already know." Mrs. Green read aloud: "Daniel Morgan Jones, Baxter Street (alley), Shawnee, retired railroad mechanic, widower, born November eleventh, 1897, Wild Stream, West Virginia. . . ." Her voice trailed off.

"What's the matter?" asked Harter.

"Wild Stream, West Virginia. That's unusual."

"Why?"

"Oh, probably nothing, but I just closed out our files on another hot-lunch client who was born in Wild Stream, West Virginia. . . . He died in a fire, too. In August. I'm always a little behind on the paperwork."

"Who was that?" asked Harter, blinking his eyes and trying to push Ace Stewart out of his mind.

"I'll get the file." Again she crossed to the cabinets, and again it didn't take her long to find what she wanted. "Simon Bowman," she said, returning.

"Never heard of him. Let me see it, please. You say he died in a fire?"

She nodded, looked down at the application, and read: "Simon Bowman, no middle name, Hays Trailer Court, Rural Route One, Shawnee, retired laborer, unmarried, born June thirteenth, 1898, Wild Stream, West Virginia."

"He lived outside the city limits, huh? I guess that's why I don't remember," said Harter.

"We're a county—not a city—agency," explained Mrs. Green. "That's one of our earlier applications. It was long before Susan Devendall's time. The file may be a trifle sketchy. We've gotten better at our record keeping."

Harter picked up the sheet of handwritten notes and read: "It is important only to provide Simon Bowman with food and essentials. He spends his Social Security check mostly on liquor. He'll pawn any items of value for drinking money. He is not a very nice man."

He turned back to Mrs. Green. "You don't know whether the fire Simon Bowman died in was an arson, do you?"

"No. I didn't know either of these gentlemen myself. I know

most of our clients only through their files—but I know their files well. That's how I remembered about Wild Stream."

"Would Susan Devendall have had any reason to visit Simon Bowman?"

"Not that I'm aware of. She didn't have anything to do with actually delivering the meals to clients." She picked up Susan's list of clients and ran down it. "Simon Bowman is certainly not here."

"Would she have had a reason to go to the Hays Trailer Court?"

"She may have. It would take me a while to find out. If you consider this a priority, I'll take her logbook home this evening and try to match up addresses."

"I'd appreciate it. I don't know what's a priority yet. It might just be coincidence, these two old men from Wild Stream dying in fires in two months. It might have nothing to do with her. I just don't know."

He handed her his card.

"I'll call you first thing in the morning, Detective."

"Thanks," he said. "These two old men are something I hadn't counted on."

"Seniors."

"What?"

"We don't call them old men and old women. We call them senior citizens, or seniors."

"Was Susan Devendall good at working with seniors?"

"I didn't have any complaints about how she actually treated people, but I certainly couldn't have given her a glowing recommendation," replied Mrs. Green. "Frankly, I was glad she quit. I'd been wondering what to do about her. She seemed to waste—or lose—a lot of time. I'd spoken to her more than once about it. How long do you imagine it would take to visit a senior and fill out one of those applications?"

"No more than an hour—maybe two if she chatted a while to build up some rapport."

"That's how I see it, Detective Harter. Yet sometimes Susan might only visit two clients in a day. It's right there in her logbook."

"She could have been making a lot of stream-bank checks," said Harter.

"Stream-bank checks?"

"Private joke."

"Well, some of us suggested she might be taking an afternoon siesta," said Mrs. Green sarcastically.

God, thought Harter, this was getting complicated. The bricks were piling up but he still hadn't found one strong enough to begin the wall with.

··· 19 ···

Sky graying, dead old men rising with the moon, Harter sat in his car.

Two old men, ordinary laborers, born in the same small town, in the last century, dead now in separate fires two months apart.

It could all just be coincidence, as he'd admitted to the Commission on Aging lady.

Could be nothing more than . . . than Simon Bowman drunk and smoking in bed . . . than Daniel Jones beaten up by a punk who had then torched his place and run outside to find there was a witness, and so he had taken her with him, beat her up, dumped her body.

Yet an alley punk would hardly have kept Susan Devendall alive for two days without a ransom note, without stripping off her gold and silver, without sexually assaulting her. Unless he was a one-hundred-percent-certified sadist.

Furthermore, the odds were good that Daniel Jones knew— or at least had known—Simon Bowman. And Susan Devendall had at least met Daniel Jones on her rounds. There was a dotted circle there that might be filled in with a little work.

Work.

Harter had tried to convince himself he wasn't lazy for not

going to the Hays Trailer Court immediately. He'd justified it by telling himself he'd see the place clearer by daylight.

Hell, hadn't he already called the state police about Bowman and the August fire? Hadn't they said the investigating trooper was off Wednesdays and would be back in the morning?

Sure, he could have called the fire marshal's office. But Caruthers had gone out the door at five sharp, and he'd bet the fire marshal had too, so he'd followed their lead. Not to head home, of course. It *was* Wednesday. He'd headed to Liz's.

Across the street, girls wearing coats over their leotards filed out of the studio and hopped in their mothers' waiting station wagons to be chauffered home to dinner. When he figured they were all gone, Harter took a last long puff and rubbed out his cigarette. He lifted the market bag off the seat, climbed out from behind the wheel, and made his way over the leaf-splattered street to the main door of the studio. The beige curtains covering the window walls of the corner building were backlit with fluorescent light. Sale signs had once hung in the huge windows, back when the building had housed a Ma & Pa grocery serving a modest portion of the west side.

Liz had been able to buy the brick structure for a song. No one had shown any interest in reopening a store in the residential neighborhood. The empty downstairs provided plenty of room for uninterrupted dancing and exercise. Upstairs was a rambling high-ceilinged apartment, complete with window seats and a view of the midtown bridge and the courthouse dome.

Opening the door, he was surprised to find her still at work. Weather Report, or some other electronic bass-heavy jazz, masterblasted out of the large speaker boxes on the far wall.

Liz was stretching on the wood floor, making occasional jerky movements to the offbeat while illustrating some elusive motion to a freckled young student who couldn't seem to find the right beat, much less perform to it.

"I'll never be able to do it," the girl almost whined.

"Sure you will. When I was twelve, there were loads of things I didn't think I'd ever master," said Liz, rather unconvincingly.

"You're a natural dancer, Miss McGee," insisted the girl. "Didn't you dance in New York when you were young?"

Liz stopped her demonstration and nodded at the girl. "I'm not so old now," she said with a hint of a smile.

"I didn't mean . . ."

"I know you didn't," said Liz—almost wearily, thought Harter. She pointed in his direction. "I'm afraid I have a visitor. You go home now and practice that movement over and over again. I'm positive you'll have it down by next week."

The girl glanced at Harter for a long instant before hurrying over to her coat hanging from a hook on the wall. Slipping it on, she almost ran past him and out the door.

"Do you think she decided I'm all right for you?" asked Harter. "I didn't mean to come in while someone was here. I thought they were all gone."

"It's just as well. I wanted her to go. She needed to get out of here. Besides, it was good she saw you. Maybe she won't think I'm such a sad old spinster."

"A pretty shapely spinster."

Liz ignored him and continued, "She tries so hard. If she only had talent. Half of my girls want to be Solid Gold dancers— wouldn't that shock their moms and dads? The other half couldn't feel the beat if they were the drum."

She switched off the tape player, then walked over to him and put her arms around his shoulders. "How are you?"

"Tired and confused," he heard himself say. He fumbled with the grocery bag and she gave him enough room to put it down on the floor. When he was standing straight again, their arms went around each other almost automatically. As they hugged, his fingers rubbed down her back until they were on her buttocks, smooth and dancer-firm under her black tights.

"Not now," she said, inching away. "I need a shower."

"Then I'll start cooking. I brought dinner," he said, picking up the groceries again.

"What are we having?"

He went through the motion of peeking in the bag. "Steaks, mushrooms, tomatoes, Italian bread."

"Red meat isn't good for you," she chided.

"The mushrooms'll make up for it. They'll make us visionaries."

"You know, I'd have thought steak and mushrooms were just what you'd have wanted for your birthday dinner Saturday— *your second birthday dinner,*" she said, crossing the dance floor to the stairs.

"We can have it again in three days. I could eat steak a couple times a week. Man is a hunter," he said, flipping off the downstairs lights before following her up. "Anyway, I don't really need another birthday dinner."

"One's fortieth birthday should be a big occasion—not something to be interrupted by a call from headquarters, not a night to be tramping around in the mud looking at corpses."

"Thirty-nine, forty-one, what's the difference? Hemingway made love morning, noon, and night when he turned fifty, just to see if he still could. Who knows if he could do the same thing at fifty-one? It wasn't the first, or worst, time I'd tramped around in the mud looking at corpses."

"Macho man," she said, leading the way down the hall to her kitchen. "I think wrapping up one decade and starting another is a big event."

"Wait till you're forty and see what I do to you."

"Do I have to wait two years to find out?"

"It'll take me that long to plan it. You know how slow I am."

She filled a glass of water from the kitchen tap, sipped at it, then, after touching his shoulder lightly, went down the hall to the bathroom.

By the time the shower water was running, he'd disposed of his jacket and gun, stuck the steaks under the broiler, decided against baked potatoes as too heavy, and begun chopping mushrooms.

He'd turned the steaks and was slicing the tomato when she returned. She went to work reaching plates down from a cabinet and he found himself putting down the sharp knife and watching the backs of her legs as her skirt swayed with her movements.

"How's your case going?" she asked abruptly as she turned around. Not waiting for an answer, she carried the plates into the small dining room off the kitchen.

Strange question, Harter said to himself. She usually didn't ask about his job, though she did listen closely when he volunteered something.

He said nothing until she came back to the kitchen and started filling water glasses at the sink. "You hardly ever say much about my cases. Why this one? I'm sure it's not just because it got in the way of dinner Saturday night."

"Partly it's your expression. You look like a wheel has fallen off and you don't have a spare. And partly, it's . . ." She carried the glasses into the other room. This time he followed her. "Partly it's because I know some of the people involved."

He leaned against the doorway and watched her take silverware from a drawer. "Who do you know?"

"Susan Devendall. I read about her in the paper. I know all the Devendalls, in fact. And a lot of their circle."

"You know Howard and the old woman?"

Liz nodded as she placed the silverware atop blue cloth napkins. "I've been to weddings, parties, and social occasions that they attended. Susan took my exercise classes now and then. Not regularly. Sometimes she'd come with a friend. I never knew when she'd show up. She paid by the class. Remember, the majority of the women in my evening classes are from the west side. Most of the girls I teach are from the west side, too."

"Who else can afford dancing lessons and exercise classes in the middle of a depression?"

"There you go again," she said.

He was immediately sorry he'd thrown a kink into whatever she'd wanted to tell him. "Forget I said it."

"It's no worse than things you've said before."

"Who were her friends?" he asked to get her back on track. "It might be helpful to talk to some of them."

"*Friends* might not be the right word. *Acquaintances* might be more like it. There was a sort of wall between Susan Devendall and most of the west-side women, even when she'd come with a group of them. You'll get to meet some of them at the Halloween party next week. You haven't forgotten, have you?"

"No," he mumbled, but in truth he had forgotten, or had tried to. He always felt out of place at parties.

"It's a costume party at the Winhams," she reminded him. "I teach their daughters. Have you thought about what you'll wear?"

"Will Howard and Amy Devendall be there?" asked Harter, ignoring her question. He didn't want to think about a costume.

"I'm sure they'd have all been there if the murder hadn't happened. Even at her age, Amy Devendall doesn't miss much."

"I can believe that. I met her yesterday for the first time. Met Howard, too. Somehow they managed to put me off for forty-eight hours. I should have seen them before, but they didn't want to be seen. The old lady is quite . . . imposing. She seems like she's had Shawnee society around her finger from the time she was a child."

"I don't know anything about her background. I don't think she's originally from Shawnee. She's the mistress of the perfect scene, though."

Harter nodded agreement, not exactly sure what he was agreeing to. He moved back in the kitchen, opened the oven, and took out the steaks. "I gather Amy Devendall wasn't fond of her daughter-in-law," he said when he realized Liz had followed him.

"True. Amy didn't approve of Susan, and Susan didn't like or approve of Amy."

"Where did Howard fit in?" asked Harter as he placed the steaks and mushrooms on a platter beside the sliced tomatoes.

"Oh, Howard can be downright charming," said Liz, opening the refrigerator. "Sometimes you can almost see what Susan originally saw in him. Away from his mother, he can come on as quite the ladies' man."

"Has he ever come on to you?" asked Harter, feeling a twinge of jealousy.

"Not seriously." She put the bread and butter on the dining room table and sat down.

"You say he's a ladies' man when he's *away* from his mother?"

"He's all propriety when she's around, like a preacher's kid."

"How long did you know Susan?"

"I'd known who she was for years. A couple of years ago some of the west-side women went on the good-health kick and began coming to aerobics classes. Like I said, she'd come once in a while. I never sensed any of the others were particularly close to her. I sensed she felt the life of a society lady was too frivolous for her. She had a job and all. She seemed to have more passion and fire than most of the others. She didn't engage much in west-side gossip. It's like some of the others only come here so they can gossip with the girls."

"Did the gossip ever involve the Devendalls?" asked Harter,

cutting into his steak, then glancing down quickly to be sure it was well done.

"The gossip involved everyone from time to time," said Liz. "You have to understand, I haven't seen Susan Devendall herself since February or March. I've only heard smatterings about her."

"Okay, you've disclaimed it enough. I'm not taking notes. Go on. Tell me what was said. You can't just bring it up and then leave me hanging."

"Oh, I could."

"I'll subpoena you."

"She was having affairs," said Liz straight out.

"And it was common knowledge?"

Liz laughed. "Sometimes these women tell each other about their own affairs."

"And it's not damaging to their reputations? Amy Devendall seemed so concerned about reputation."

"It all depends on who the affair is with. Amy Devendall might even have been behind some of the rumors."

"Why would she do that?"

"To give Howard some cover." She looked at Harter over a raised forkful of mushrooms. "If Susan was running around, then Howard's philandering seemed justified. Don't you see?"

"I guess," said Harter. He was slightly amazed that Liz's daily work put her as deeply into a well of intrigues as his own. In the years they'd seen each other, they'd never discussed west-side affairs and gossip.

"Understand, it's a small circle we're talking about," she explained. "When I say something was common knowledge, I don't mean the man on the street knows it or that you should. Half the women in my classes had their flings, and the other half had wandering husbands. Sometimes the halves overlapped. They all have plenty of money and lots of free afternoons."

"Afternoon siesta," said Harter, remembering Mrs. Green's remark.

"What?"

"Just a thought. . . . So Howard was running around, too?"

"I'd say they were evenly matched. What I'd guess is that Amy spread the word of Susan's unfaithfulness to explain Howard's. All's fair in love and war."

"I never believed that."

"It doesn't matter what *you* believe."

"You know the names of any people that either of them might have been involved with?"

"Just one with any degree of certainty."

"Well, tell me."

"Charles Whitford Canley."

"The congressman?"

"The congressman."

"I guess it was Susan and not Howard."

"Don't get nasty," said Liz.

"So what's the story?"

"Congressman Canley is a widower. His wife died last year. Since then he's been spending a lot of time at a farm west of Shawnee owned by the Whitfords, his mother's family. It's a big spread, used to be a virtual plantation. Between staying at the farm and frequently visiting Shawnee to campaign this year, he's been in the area almost as much as in Washington. They say Susan Devendall volunteered time as a campaign worker. Of course, she and Canley had known each other socially a long time. The two got entwined."

"But if she was a social worker . . . if she had this streak of social consciousness I keep hearing about . . . she couldn't have found a less socially conscious congressman to work for."

"The Devendalls have always been big supporters of the Canleys. I also heard Susan quit her job after some bad scene with a welfare case."

Ace Stewart. The "attempted rape." Was Ace telling the truth? *Had* she come on to him? Was she looking for a lover? Had he scared her into Canley's arms?

"You don't know when she started sleeping with the congressman, do you?" Harter asked her.

"The rumors started late in the spring, just before the primary election."

He nodded. It jibed. "Why didn't you ever tell me about them?"

"Why should I have?"

"Do you know Canley?"

"I've met him."

"Charming fellow?"

"If you don't think about politics. He's quite a party-goer. If we go to the Winhams for Halloween, he'll probably be there."

"I can't wait ten days to meet him," Harter thought out loud.

"Call him up in Washington," she said. "A congressman's not hard to find."

"I may," said Harter. Then: "You said the Devendalls were always big political supporters of the Canleys. Did the affair change things?"

"I doubt it," answered Liz after a moment's thought. "On the west side, politics are kept carefully separated from the rest of life."

"Hypocrites."

"Pragmatists," she corrected. To let him know she'd told him all she could, or would, she glanced over at the clock on the wall and said, "We still have time to get to a movie out at the mall."

"Okay," he said without much zest.

Usually he loved movies, the bigger-than-life action. But he didn't really feel like it tonight, didn't particularly want to watch another mystery unfold.

He watched as Liz got up from the table and removed the plates. He watched her dancer's body, her long legs, as she headed to the kitchen.

He hoped the movie would be a comedy, a sexy comedy that would be over quickly so they could come back to the apartment and climb into bed. The same bed.

Not like Susan and Howard Devendall.

··· 20 ···

If Hays Trailer Court wasn't the ugliest spot in the universe, it was close enough to be in the running. It sprawled up a straggly shale hillside about three miles south of Shawnee. Some land-use expert on the take had apparently decided the hill was worthless for anything but propping up trailers, figured Harter. Only scroungy pastel tin cans were allowed—the smaller and rustier, the better.

On the other side of the county road was Hays Salvage Yard. Its sign boasted 189 ACRES OF AUTO PARTS.

Whether the spread of bashed-in cars and half-dismantled trucks was uglier than the slope of trailers was a toss-up. Harter sided with the trailer court. For starters, the junkyard's sign looked half-professional, but the trailer-court sign looked as if it had been created by a second-grader who'd been given his first gallon of thin black paint and a stick to use as a brush. Beneath HAYS TRAILOR CORT was the message *Aply at salvagE YarD*.

The man in the junkyard office was friendly enough. He listened to Harter and then said, "You want to see Phil, that's who. He runs that place over there." Stepping to the back door, he bellowed, *"Phil! Phil! There's a cop here to see you!"*

Phil Hays turned out to be a chubby bald fellow in a gray windbreaker and checkered pants. Harter decided that, with proper attire, he could have done business on Sinclair Lewis' Main Street.

"City cop, huh? You're out of your jurisdiction, aren't you? I thought you detectives always worked in pairs, like on 'Dragnet,'" said Hays.

"Think of me as a loner. The state police told me it would be all right to ask a few questions. They couldn't spare a trooper to send around with me."

"What's the big deal? Nothing going on here."

No stolen vehicles on your lot? Harter wanted to ask. Instead, he said, "I'm looking into a couple deaths. Last week an old man died in an arson in town. He may have known the old man who died in the fire out here. It's just a routine check to see if there's a connection."

"Looking for a conspiracy, huh? I can't believe anyone would conspire to burn up Simon Bowman. That fire wasn't an arson. If you ask me, Simon's kerosene tank leaked. It was right outside his trailer and he could have dropped a match or something. I tell those goddamned people to be careful all the time. My fire insurance has tripled since the fire. You can't make it up on what I charge for those places."

"You rented the trailer to Bowman?"

"No, he owned his, just rented the lot. I don't know where he got the money to buy it. Showed up here one day right after I started the court. Bought the trailer in cash. He paid me twenty-five bucks a month for the space."

"How long did he live there?"

"From about 1965 until he died."

"You must have known him pretty well."

"Well enough to know when to go collect my rent from him. There were only two times a month when he had money—when the Social Security checks came out and then around the twentieth, when he'd get a little extra from someplace. If you weren't there to collect at the right time, he'd drink the money up. Funny thing, he gave up drinking a year or two ago. Straightened up after all those years. Who'd have figured that?"

"You mean he gave up the bottle in his early eighties?"

Hays nodded. "Must have started worrying about his soul. Reverend Sam Knotts must have scared him to death."

"Who's that?"

"Sam Knotts runs a church back near the Shawnee line on Route Forty-three. You had to pass it to get here. He started with just a revival tent and built up a complex. Good businessman. He goes through the trailer court evangelizing fairly regularly. Simon probably drank for fifty years before Sam Knotts put a stop to it."

"What'd Bowman ever do for a living?"

"Got me. Never talked about it. I think he worked for the canal in the old days and maybe the railroad a while. He didn't talk that much about anything. All I ever knew him to do was drink, until he got religion. I always wondered if he had a guardian angel. He never ran completely downhill. Like I said, he paid for that trailer in cash."

"No family?"

"None I know of."

"Did he ever mention anyone named Daniel Jones, someone he might have known back in Wild Stream, West Virginia?"

"Was he from there? I didn't know that. I don't think I ever heard him mention a friend named Daniel Jones. He never mentioned any friends."

"Anybody come to visit him?"

"Just Reverend Sam and the COA hot-lunch van. Sunday mornings, Knotts would send someone up to get him to bring him down to church. Sam's real organized about stuff like that. He runs his church tight."

"How'd Bowman get around the rest of the time?"

"Bummed rides or hitchhiked. He didn't go far. You wouldn't have wanted Simon behind the wheel of a car."

"Were you around the night of the fire?"

"I live across town," said Hays. "I came over when they called me, but the place was gone by then. Simon was baked inside. It was a Thursday night. I remember because it was my wife's card-party night."

"Thursday, August fifth, according to police reports."

"That must be right. You cops are always right, aren't you?"

Harter resisted the urge to punch Hays' face. "You mind if I go up and look at where Bowman lived?"

"Suit yourself. Nothing to see. The trailer's gone." Hays went over to the window, bent the venetian blinds, and pointed to a spot partway up the hill. "There's still some rubble. You'll find it."

"Us cops always find it," said Harter.

A few minutes later he did find it, but Hays was right. There was nothing to see—except a scenic view of 189 acres of broken automotive dreams. According to the state police, there'd been little to see on the night of the fire, too. Everything had been inconclusive from the start.

Nor had the Commission on Aging been much help. Mrs. Green had called him at nine sharp. She'd gone through Susan Devendall's logs. She'd found no reason for her to have visited the trailer park.

Trailer park. What a misuse of the language. Harter wondered how much Hays charged for the air.

Suddenly, he sensed that someone was staring at him from the window of the pink can next to the rubble of what had once been Simon Bowman's home. The trailer was little more than the type of thing campers took out for the weekend. Harter walked over and knocked on the door. Though he was sure someone was inside, no one answered. He knocked again, waited, and knocked a third time. He finally gave up, climbed into his car, and, cussing the rutted road, left Hays Trailer Court.

The old men were nagging at him.

He didn't want to get sidetracked, but . . . .

But . . .

Kerosene and Wild Stream, West Virginia. . . .

··· 21 ···

When he spotted the church, he pulled off the highway and into the parking lot, coming to a stop among pickup trucks that seemed to belong to the construction workers busy putting up a large brick building in a field nearby.

For a while, he sat in the car, watching the construction activity, debating whether it was worth talking to the Reverend Sam Knotts, whose name was proudly displayed on the marquee. He knew *marquee* wasn't the right word, but he had no idea what else to call the bulletin board in front of the white building. It was one of those metal contraptions with changeable letters. Today it announced that Sam Knotts' sermon on Sunday would be "The City Built by God."

Surely not the Hays Trailor Cort, thought Harter.

According to the marquee, Knotts' True Church Of God kept a bustling schedule: Sunday school, two Sunday morning services, a Sabbath evening adult class, a Monday night "Faith Workshop" (whatever that was), and a Wednesday evening hymn sing. SINNERS INVITED read the bottom line of white plastic letters.

Finally Harter hauled himself out of his car and went to the side door of the church. "Anyone here?" he called as he stepped onto a ramp that led into the innards of the spic-and-span church building. Cleanliness is next to Godliness, he remembered.

"Praise the Lord, you've come," answered a male voice. Before long, a man came out of one of the doorways along the carpeted hallway.

"Reverend Sam Knotts?"

"Called and answered," said the man cheerfully.

Harter had seen such evangelical good cheer in older ministers, but found it slightly odd in so young a man. Sam Knotts couldn't have been more than thirty-five. Well over six feet tall and sturdily built, he looked like a football tackle. He wore his red hair styled and his muscular frame was covered with a yellow sports jacket, no tie this non-service weekday.

"My name is Edward Harter. I'm a detective with the Shawnee Police Department."

"Something wrong?" asked Knotts, extending a big hand.

"Not exactly. I'm working a case and was told you might have known Simon Bowman."

Knotts nodded his red head. "Is the trailer fire still being investigated?"

"Actually, we're looking for a pattern in some recent fires. There may be nothing to it."

"*Some* fires?" asked Knotts.

"Yeah."

"I'm not sure how I can help, but come in."

Knotts led Harter down the hall and turned into the room he'd come out of. He motioned for Harter to sit on a low orange couch beside a bookcase filled with religious-looking volumes. Knotts sat right next to him, not a foot away. People who didn't allow you room always made Harter tense, but he tried not to show it.

"As I hear it, Simon Bowman had been an alcoholic most of his life."

"I'd say that's accurate," said Knotts. "I worked very hard to help him kick it. Little by little, he opened up to me as I tried to prepare his heart for salvation. Building confidence is difficult, as I'm sure you know, Detective Harter. I remember well the day I saved Simon. You can see it in a person's eyes—you can see that leap they make when they give themselves over to Christ. He began crying and confessing and went on and on for hours. We prayed and prayed together in his meager trailer."

Harter wanted to ask what Simon Bowman had "confessed," but thought better of it and simply said, "If he gave up drinking after all those years, it sounds like it worked."

"It always works," said Knotts. "It's not a game. It's a matter of readying the person to accept the Lord. God will forgive anything if you are willing to start anew, Detective."

Harter felt more uncomfortable. Bad enough to be sitting so close to the preacher without having the soul-saving faucet turned on. The flowery speech didn't match the tough body.

"I take it you saw a good bit of Bowman after that?"

"He began coming to church on Sundays, and I'd always stop in and see him on my visits to the trailer court. There are so many lost souls there. Some of them I've yet to reach. I know they're inside, but they won't answer the door."

"When was the last time you saw Bowman?"

"I believe it was the Sunday-morning service before the fire. One of my volunteers had gone up to get him and bring him to church. I think I probably saw him the week before that, too. I usually visit the trailer court toward the end of the month, and he died early in August, as I recall."

"That's right. When you, uh, talked to him, he didn't ever mention family or close friends, did he?"

"Nobody he still had contact with. Simon was a very lonely man. Most of the people he once knew are gone."

"I'm specifically interested in whether he ever mentioned an elderly man named Daniel Jones or a social worker named Susan Devendall," said Harter, watching Knotts' face carefully.

The preacher showed no emotion. "I don't recall anything about a Daniel Jones. Occasionally he'd refer to someone he knew when he was young or whom he had worked with, but the names didn't stick with me. I know he didn't mention Susan Devendall."

"Why are you so sure?"

"I'd have remembered. I knew her."

"You knew her?"

"Not very well, but I knew her. Her husband, Howard, has done legal work for the church—mostly things to help us maintain our tax-exempt status when we started new projects. His mother, Amy Devendall, is quite a character."

"Yeah," mumbled Harter, surprised. "Are the Devendalls members of your church?" He found it hard to picture Amy Devendall and Simon Bowman sharing a pew.

"I believe they attend West Side Episcopal, but they're concerned, generous people. From my conversations with them, I know they're worried about the moral fabric of this country."

"Tell me how you met Susan Devendall," asked Harter.

"I believe I first met her at her husband's office one day, and then we all had lunch together. Later I ran into all three of them at functions for Congressman Canley. Susan's murder was such a senseless tragedy. I called on Mrs. Devendall to give her my condolences."

"How did you size her up?" asked Harter awkwardly.

"I beg your pardon?"

"What was your impression of Susan Devendall?"

"I knew her husband better through business, and I talked more easily with her mother-in-law. I'm not the person to tell you about her. Confidentially, I wouldn't say she led an immoral life, but I know her lifestyle worried her family." Knotts halted and tapped Harter's knee. "You're just fishing, Detective, aren't you?"

"Did Simon Bowman know her?" asked Harter, more uncomfortable than ever.

"I don't know why he would have," answered Knotts. "I told you he never mentioned her."

"When was the last time you saw her?"

"I'd say it was at a picnic rally for Congressman Canley in July. Yes, I'm positive that's when it was. There aren't many politicians, you know, with the congressman's backbone. I admire him greatly. I had dinner with him last Thursday night, in fact."

Thursday night. The night of the fire, the night of Susan's disappearance.

"Where was the dinner?" asked Harter.

"At Richard Baum's church in town. Our ministerial group gave the congressman an award for standing up for basic American values."

Thinking of what Liz had told him the night before, Harter ignored the testimonial for Canley and asked, "Did anything unusual happen that evening?"

"No," said Knotts, sounding put off by the question. "We ate. I got a chance to encourage him to support legislation that would give tax deductions for tuition for private and religious schools. It's important for people to be able to choose how they educate their children, Detective."

"That all?"

"He left us rather early for another engagement. After he'd gone, our group spent a few hours in fellowship. On the way home, I stopped here to check on the construction site, as I do each night. We had some vandalism early on. I came by the church about ten, then went home."

"What is it you're building out there?"

"A Christian academy. Didn't you notice the sign? The school is the next step in my dream, and a very expensive step I might add. The congregation has really dug into their pockets and we've solicited some outside donations. It's a crucial part of my ministry to be able to educate children properly—away from drugs, evolution textbooks, secular humanism. They'll be raised as we were, Detective. Prayer, the fundamentals, proper discipline. Spare the rod and spoil the child, as they say. You know, Simon Bowman was especially excited about the school. It's a pity he didn't live to see construction begin. He pledged to donate all the money he'd once spent on liquor. He believed that by raising up the children right, they wouldn't stray as he had. Mercifully, he was one of the strays I managed to collect."

"Huh," said Harter, unable to think of anything else to say.

A few minutes later, outside Knotts' church, he stared again at the school in the works.

FUTURE HOME OF OUR CHRISTIAN ACADEMY
Made possible by friends of
The True Church of God
and by a donation in Memory of A.L.

Sam Knotts, pastor

A.L.?

Probably another old alcoholic that Knotts had redeemed.

But one with more moolah than Simon Bowman.

Christ, the job could make you mean. Sometimes he wondered why the hell he was a cop.

Liz would never fully understand.

...

JACK REESE

...

··· 22 ···

You run down to the bottom floor of the old house and see a wooden table with a tall candle and the candle falls over and the table starts to burn like paper and I run over and try to smother the flames with your bare hands.

Noise of a burglar upstairs.

Run up to the second floor and see a table with a candle and the candle falls and the table starts to burn and you run over and try to smother flames with my hands.

Run up third floor see table candle falls table burns run try to smother flames with bare hands.

I would wake up and try to shake the dream, but when I imagined it had passed it would only be replaced by visions of Daniel's blazing house on that alley night:

I am standing outside the streetlight circle, in the stretched gray alley shadows, leaning against the Ford, watching the house burn, unable to do anything. Or I try and I run into her damn car and lose track of what's going on.

A guilt no preacher could bring about in me.

Should have turned her down when I saw how the sessions were shaping up.

Should have found some way to help Daniel.

Should have told Harter the whole truth when he came the first time.

I kept telling myself I hadn't really lied.

Stared at his card countless times.

Monday at the towpath I'd almost come clean, almost poured it out. But I hadn't. For some reason, I hadn't.

"You come here often?" he'd asked, suspicious of his suspect.

"I wanted to see it," I'd answered, backing away from the full story.

After we'd split up, after he'd driven off, I'd wandered about, trying to decide what to do.

I'd walked over the bridge to the abandoned cardboard box factory and then the sign caught my eye.

Sign on the factory, near the spot where her abductor, her killer, had deposited her body.

I clicked the picture.

Later, watching it come up in the darkroom tray, I'd almost called him.

But Harter must have known about the building. He was the cop. He looked like he knew more than he showed. Or were all detectives like that? I'd never been head-to-head with a detective before.

He'd left me feeling stripped down to the itchy essentials, like being on stage wearing only a loincloth, before ten thousand pairs of hard eyes—like his—with spotlights illuminating every bump of me. As vulnerable as Susan Maddox Devendall had been before my camera.

And the dream kept returning.

I hadn't lied.

Day after day of nervous waiting. Waiting for him to come back. I *knew* Harter would come back.

I got everything ready for him. Put all my pictures in a pile, in order. Every one that could be considered evidence. Every one that could show what I'd been doing the week before.

But no Harter.

Wednesday night I tried to call him. They offered to take my name and message at the police department. I said I'd call back. I tried to get him at home. He wasn't there.

Thursday morning I tried again. He mustn't have gone home the night before. At headquarters, a guy who said he was a detective asked me to leave a message again. I'll call back, I said. I didn't want to talk to anyone but Harter. Didn't want to get other cops involved.

I kept staring at the pile of photos, wishing I could fill him in, remind him of the sign, tell him why Susan Devendall had called me the night of the fire.

I was innocent, even if he made me feel like a cheap pornographer.

"I thought maybe you took pictures for *Playboy* or something," he'd said Sunday evening.

You're the only one who knew both victims.

Run

Candle falls.

Table burns.

Try to smother flames.

Bare hands.

If only the guilt would subside and the dream would begin to dissolve.

If only the fire trucks would come.

··· 23 ···

"The son of a bitch, the son of a bitch," Tattoo was repeating as I stepped into the kitchen at lunchtime Thursday. I hoped he wasn't talking about me.

"It's only politics, Henry," said May.

"What's the matter?"

"A piece in the paper has him all lit up," she told me.

"I'm innocent," I insisted.

"Look at this," Tattoo ordered. He shoved *The News* across the table at me, almost knocking a soup bowl to the floor in the process.

CONGRESSMAN SEEKS
RAILROAD INVESTIGATION

"I intend to expose a national scandal," Congressman Charles Whitford Canley had announced at a press conference in Washington on Wednesday. Canley claimed to have observed an upsurge in train wrecks.

A passenger train had left the rails in Pennsylvania in September, injuring a dozen people. Three chemical cars had ruptured in a Texas crash in July, forcing the evacuation of two small towns. EPA was still on the scene, spending bundles of tax dollars.

Just the previous Tuesday, Canley reported, he'd been in Shawnee when a freight train loaded with new trucks had derailed near town.

The danger was nationwide, but Shawnee—with its railroad economy—was especially vulnerable, he'd said.

The wrecks destroyed valuable goods, injured ordinary people, shook the public confidence in rail transportation, forced higher insurance rates.

Canley was sure he knew what was at the bottom of the accidents. The union bosses wouldn't face up to it, but it was drugs. Not faulty equipment, not bad tracks, not the nature of rail transport, but *illegal drugs*. High, speeding engineers who didn't pay attention to signal lights. Bombed-out mechanics who didn't care about the quality of their work.

The evil of drugs, brought into American society by the hippies and social anarchists of the 1960s, was undermining the railroad industry while union leaders looked the other way, claimed Canley. So he'd called for a congressional investigation.

The News reported the congressman would discuss the issue further at a news conference in the Shawnee courthouse on Friday.

I looked at Tattoo. "Sounds like our honorable representative has found a hot one for the last couple of weeks before the election."

"How can he get off saying Harry Bryson is a drug addict?" said Tattoo.

"Got me. That's why I'm not a politician."

"Goddamn newspaper puts trash like this on the front page and not a word about who killed Daniel."

He shot a challenging stare my way to let me know he still

expected me to call Metling and get the inside dope, but he said nothing. After a while, he rose from the table and stomped up the steps.

"You want a bowl of vegetable soup?" asked May, ignoring his anger.

"No. I came over to go down to the food bank with you."

"So Reverend Ruffing asked you about taking pictures?"

"Yeah. I told him I can't promise whether they'll get in the paper."

"Just do your best." She removed the empty soup bowls from the table and took them to the sink. "Let me do the dishes and wash my face, then we'll go."

I watched her at the sink for a minute, then went upstairs to see if Tattoo had cooled off. He was sitting in his chair, stuffing a chaw of tobacco in his mouth.

"I thought you gave that up."

"Took it up again."

"May must be happy."

He stayed grumpy and didn't answer.

She hated it when he chewed, hated that stale moist tobacco odor in the air, hated it when he spit into the stained white spittoon at his feet, and missed. I pictured him younger, two-armed, gabbing and chewing on the porch with my grandfather, the two of them spitting their brown streams toward the street. When they'd run low, they'd send me down to Bernhardt's for fresh Mail Pouch, tossing in an extra nickel for candy.

I heard May's steps on the stairs. "Ready?" she asked when she came into the room.

I got up from the sofa. "You want to walk or ride?"

"Let's walk. It's a nice day," she said, slipping on her coat.

Heading down the hill, I was afraid she'd ask me about the detective or the murders. I hadn't discussed any of it with her and didn't know what she'd heard from Tattoo. But she was quiet until we passed the Listons' apartment house and their watchdog barked. The Listons had always had a vicious German shepherd. We believed they took the ones the police couldn't trust.

"You remember when their dog attacked you?" asked May.

"Sure. I was about ten. I was running down the sidewalk and it came off the porch after me. My sweater gave when its teeth pulled at it. Wasn't until I got home and my mother saw my shirt was ripped under the sweater that we realized how close I'd come to having my arm ripped off. It may be unAmerican, but I've never been able to stand dogs since."

"I don't like them neither, and Tattoo doesn't trust cats, so we never had neither. I feed him and he pets me."

We crossed the Avenue.

"You think you're going to stay in Shawnee?" she asked.

I debated lying but gave her an honest answer. "I don't know. A lot of things would make life look different—if I had a more regular income, if I had someone to date . . ." I stopped myself from adding, *If the murders hadn't happened.*

"Used to be that young fellows would meet girls at church," she said. "I don't know what it is, though. Young people today don't seem to go to church, unless they catch religion and end up holy rollers."

"I don't know what it is either," I said, keeping my thoughts to myself.

"You have to twist Henry's arm to get him in a church. I gave up on it a long time ago."

We crossed Thomas Street, walked past the front door of the church, and went up the brick walkway that led to the side entrance.

The Sunday school room didn't look a whole lot different than the last time I'd been in it. But on a Thursday afternoon, there was no piano player to chord out "In the Garden." Every available surface—the piano bench, the folding chairs, the Sunday school tables—was filled with cartons of food.

As May hung up her coat, I scouted out the selection. Spaghetti, tomato sauce, cereal, flour, bread.

"No filet mignon," said Reverend Joe Ruffing, coming up behind me. "Mostly generic staples. We have to think about getting the most food for the money. Thank you for coming."

"I promised I would. So how does this thing work?"

"May sits at the table over by the door and has people fill out an application—things like how many are in the family and their average monthly income. She decides how much they need. She's a pro at sifting them out. She knows most of the people from the neighborhood, and she's good at reading the ones she doesn't know. We can only afford to help the really needy."

"Not just Methodists?"

"Of course not," said Ruffing. "All sorts of people. Ones waiting for their unemployment compensation to start. Ones without unemployment, trying to stay off welfare. Transients on their way south. Elderly people whose Social Security check ran out. Cases referred by the Department of Human Services. There's not much outright fraud."

"There's your first customer," I said, nodding at a disheveled woman in her seventies who stood in the doorway with an empty shopping bag in her hand.

"She's a regular," said Ruffing. "Take any pictures you want. Try to avoid faces on any that'll end up in the newspaper."

"I usually do," I said, remembering my reluctance to photograph faces at the cheese-and-butter line at the theater.

Leaving me alone, Ruffing crossed the room to greet the people who were filing in line behind the woman.

There was a black girl with an infant in her arms. She seemed hardly big enough to hold the baby.

There was a second old lady, her stockings bagging at the ankles.

There was a couple—him bearded, her with long straight blond hair—both in shabby blue jeans. They might have gone to East Shawnee High with me.

I turned away from the faces and fiddled with the camera so I'd be ready for the first shot. The lady didn't ask any questions or appear to mind when I snapped her putting a box of soup noodles in her brown bag. I moved behind her, framing her small body hunched over the canned goods.

Click.

A hand gripped the plastic wrap of a loaf of bread.

Click.

The baby's eyes stared out at me, its head resting on its mother's shoulder as she picked up a box of spaghetti.

Click.

The mother's hand grasped a white flour bag.

Click.

The couple were more self-conscious. As they made their way along the row of folding chairs loaded with boxes, his eyes never left me. I found myself zeroing in on the food and not them.

Click.

Down the line, other pairs of hands reached for containers of food.

Click.

More people, more hands.

Click. Click.

"There's a man outside wants to see you," said May, tapping my arm to bring me out of my camera-clicking trance.

I glanced toward the door but all I could see past the food cartons were more people waiting their turn. Then I saw Joe Ruffing's thin back. He was talking to someone.

Harter.

When I joined them on the brick walkway, they were in the middle of a discussion about a minister or church. It was the first time I'd seen Joe Ruffing show any discernible anger.

"He's built his empire in the last four or five years," he was telling Harter. "First the church, now the school. I've heard he came from Virginia originally. I don't know for sure. I've never had a real conversation with him. I stay away from Sam Knotts' ilk."

"How about Simon Bowman?" Harter asked.

"Draws a blank." Ruffing looked my way. "Did you ever hear of him, Jack?"

"Simon Bowman?"

"Daniel Jones never mentioned him to you?"

"I don't think so. If he was an old railroader or something, Tattoo's the one you ought to ask."

"I just came from his place," said Harter, staring directly at me. "He told me I could find you here."

"And he didn't know this Simon Bowman?"

"He might retrieve something from his memory yet," answered Harter, clearly watching his words. "He seems to think Bowman might have been a scab in the twenties or thirties and had a poor reputation among the union men. You know how that goes, I'm sure. I just figured maybe Jones had told you some story about him, or about a scab he grew up with."

I looked at the detective and he looked at me. Neither of us was anxious to get down to hard-core business while Ruffing was standing there. I knew Harter was full of questions. What he didn't know was that I was ready to tell him everything I'd done, from the moment Susan Devendall had stepped namelessly on my porch until he'd come to see me Sunday.

"You walking?" Harter finally asked, tired of waiting.

"Yeah." I looked at Ruffing. "I'll bring some pictures by in a couple of days. You can choose the ones you like. Tell May I'll come down and pick her up if she calls me."

"I'll get her home," said Ruffing.

"My car's across the street." Harter pointed as we started down the walk.

"I . . . I . . ."

"What?" he asked, opening his car door.

"I've been trying to call you." I climbed in and sat next to him.

"About what?" He turned the key and the engine roared.

"I . . . I've got some photos you'll be interested in."

"Of what?"

I was still unclear exactly where to start. I decided to save the bulk of the story until I'd convinced him I was on his side.

"Several things. One of them I took Monday—after you left me near the old box factory. It's a sign on the wall there. . . . You do know who owns the factory building?"

He shook his head no as he turned right into the alley.

"Howard P. Devendall," I told him. "Isn't that her husband?"

"That's her husband all right," he said, not showing half the interest I'd expected.

"Doesn't it mean something?"

"Might or it might not," he said, parking near my Ford. "It's a small town. They're a prominent family. They own a lot. What else have you got on your mind?"

"It's going to take me a while," I answered.

"I've got a while," said Harter.

He was a hard man to read. I didn't know whether I'd learn to decipher his nuances or not.

"What other pictures have you got?" he asked as we climbed the back porch steps.

Inside, I handed the whole pile over to him without comment. I turned on the burner under the coffeepot as he sat at the kitchen table and silently flipped through the prints.

When I handed him his cup, he was studying her intensely. There she was, alive, the previous Wednesday night, striking her Marilyn Monroe pose, her made-up face looking boldly at the lens—*at me*—at him—her body inside the pink fifties dress, her high heels hooked onto a stool rung.

"Not exactly Matthew Brady photojournalism," he said, lifting the hot coffee to his lips.

"No, I guess not."

"So do we play Twenty Questions or are you going to tell me?"

I told him everything I should have told him the first night but was afraid to.

I'm only human.

I wanted him to know I was no murderer.

...

EDWARD HARTER

...

··· 24 ···

From where he stood, Harter had a view of Charles Whitford Canley's left profile—not the congressman's most photogenic side. The news photographers and the TV crew from Bartlesburg were set up on the opposite end of the circuit courtroom and were able to capture his best side, the one in his campaign posters.

Harter might not have noticed how different Canley's left side was from his right if he hadn't spent a long time studying Jack Reese's photo of the politician accepting the evangelists' award for moral courage. Canley had managed to tilt his chin leftward before Reese had snapped. The chin almost poked Reverend Sam Knotts—who had been patting him on the back. *Good job, Congressman.*

In fact, from the rear of the brightly lit courtroom, Harter might not have even recognized Canley. It was as if someone had drawn a line down the middle of the congressman's head. His right side was smiling, but on the left his smile seemed to curve downward into more of a smirk. His right eye was alert, his left squinting. Canley's graying black hair was full and combed straight back on the right, but was receding on the left side of his part. Harter guessed that anyone with a perfectly symmetrical face was an oddity, but Canley's was so asymmetrical you might almost believe he was two people. "Stop projecting your animosity," Liz would have told him.

He thought back to what she'd told him two nights before, and tried to see the charming party-goer in Canley, the man who had appealed to Susan Devendall. But all he could really see was a politician talking off the top of his head about dope rings and the deterioration of the American work ethic.

Harter imagined many of the young railroaders smoked a joint now and then, but he wasn't convinced they were all junkies. People like Canley conveniently forgot how hard the old men drank, how they used to carry flasks, how Victorian ladies became morphine addicts, how the saloons along the canal were once wild and woolly.

"I don't mean to leave the impression that I'm singling out any one railroad or any one incident," Canley had said.

Then why talk about specific wrecks? wondered Harter.

Harter could understand why Tattoo had been ranting against Canley when he'd stopped by on Thursday afternoon. The old railroader had waved the newspaper so madly that it had slipped out of his hand and flown across the room, landing on the daybed.

The reporters spurred Canley on with questions, but Harter barely listened, finding himself surveying the courtroom instead. Of course, he'd been in it many times, testifying for the state or presenting his evidence to the grand jury in the privacy of the adjoining jury room. The jury room would be the perfect spot to interrogate Canley, he decided.

The photographers' flashes were lighting up Canley's face, erasing the traces of wrinkles. Harter guessed the show was about over. He thought someone ought to tell the judge it destroyed the sanctity of the courtroom to allow snollygosters to hold press conferences in it when court wasn't in session.

Some of the people began to leave. Others circled around the congressman to have a personal word. Harter slowly made his way through the spectator benches toward the front and came to a stop at the back of the clump of people, watching to be sure Canley didn't slip out on him.

Finally the TV crew packed up and the last reporter backed away. Canley picked up his speech from the lawyer's table, folded it neatly, and stuck it in the inside pocket of his slick blue suitcoat.

Harter approached. "Congressman, I'd like to speak to you if I may." He put the evidence envelopes under his arm and showed Canley his badge.

"Shawnee City Police, eh? Harter?"

"Right." *At least he could read.*

"Is there a bill before Congress you're interested in? I've always been a strong voice for law and order."

"No, I'd like to ask you some questions about a case."

"A case?"

"Susan Devendall's murder."

"Terrible thing," said Canley as if he meant it. "One reason I came to town was to go to her memorial service tomorrow. I'm a friend of the family. I've known Amy and Howard most of my life, though I didn't know Susan and the Maddox family as well."

Harter searched for the proper attack. He finally said, "That's not exactly what I've heard, Congressman."

"What *have* you heard?" challenged Canley, his voice rising.

"Some people think you were a very close friend of Susan Devendall, an intimate friend," pushed Harter. "Maybe we can sit down and talk about it."

He pointed the evidence envelopes toward the jury room. At first he wasn't sure Canley would take the suggestion, but, almost scowling, the congressman at last turned and went inside.

"I asked what you'd heard," demanded Canley after the door was shut and they were seated around the jury table.

"The word from the west side is that you've been seeing Susan Devendall for months."

"Who told you that?"

"I thought, if you did know her well, you might have some ideas on what happened to her." That was about as diplomatic as he could be, as diplomatic as he got.

Canley was obviously irritated. "The tongues on the west side never stop wagging, do they?"

Harter shrugged.

Canley didn't speak for a while. When he did, he calmly said, "Okay, I'll level with you. But get this straight. If anything I tell you ever hits the press, your ass is worse than mud. The mayor and police chief are beholden to me on more than one count. I'm no first-term novice. Most importantly, I had nothing to do with Susan's death."

"So?"

"What?"

"So tell me. I haven't heard you say anything yet."

"Why don't you forget about the chip on your shoulder and try asking an intelligent question, Harter?" snapped Canley.

"When did you last see Susan Devendall?"

"Wednesday night of last week. She came out to my farm and we had a late dinner together."

"I take it that wasn't the first time she'd been out to your farm."

"She'd been there many times since spring. She was there last Tuesday night, too. I'd called her Sunday from Washington and told her I'd cleared a few days for campaigning around Shawnee. I suggested it was time we plan a trip we'd talked about. I got into town Tuesday afternoon and she came out for dinner. She brought a photo for her passport. I was going to take care of the rest of the arrangements."

"A photo like this?" asked Harter. He opened the top envelope, pulled out a bunch of Reese's prints, and handed a head shot across the table.

Canley barely glanced at it. "Yeah."

"What was this trip you two were going to take?"

"We were going to Europe in November, after the election. She was going to tell Howard she needed some time to herself to decide what she was going to do."

"And what was she going to do?"

Canley flashed anger again. "How the hell do I know? It was all just an excuse for her to get away. We talked about, maybe, her leaving him, but I wasn't sure."

"Sure of what?"

"What it would mean politically."

And this was the man with the moral backbone that Sam Knotts and the other preachers so admired, thought Harter.

"How long had you been involved with her?" he asked.

"I don't like that word—*involved*," said Canley. "I'm not sure what business it is of yours, anyway. It's got nothing to do with her murder."

"Look, I'm not trying to embarrass you, Congressman. I'm trying to figure out what happened to Susan Devendall."

"We'd been seeing each other since May. She went to work for my campaign and we hit it off. She was at loose ends at the time. She'd had a bad time at work. . . ."

"An attempted rape?"

"So you've heard the story?"

"Several times. Amy Devendall told me first."

"Amy's a colossal bitch. She's probably the one who told you about Susan and me. We figured she'd spread rumors about us.

Susan never did get along with Amy. Howard's a eunuch—Amy's the one with the balls in the family."

Wondering if rumors were still rumors if they were true, Harter asked, "Did Amy or Howard Devendall know about this planned trip?"

"I wouldn't think so. I can't imagine Susan told them before we'd worked out the details. Howard was supposed to be in Pittsburgh all last week, so I don't see how he'd have known. That's why Susan was able to spend Tuesday and Wednesday nights with me."

"Did she stay all night?"

Canley glared at him. "She never did. She always wanted Amy to know she was home in the morning."

"Tuesday and Wednesday nights were the only times you saw her last week?"

"Yeah, and Wednesday we didn't get together until after nine because I'd been out stumping in the country all day."

"What was she wearing?"

Canley closed his eyes and pursed his lips. "I don't see what that has to do with anything."

"This?" asked Harter, holding up a photo from the Wednesday pink-dress session.

"Yeah." Again Canley scarcely looked at the picture. "You don't have to show me any more photos, Harter. I know what she looked like. I've got pictures of her myself—ones I took and ones she sent me after I'd be gone in Washington for a few weeks. What of it?"

"How about this?" Harter opened the other evidence envelope and slid the jewelry onto the table.

Canley glanced at the pile of gleaming metal. "We bought that stuff at a summer festival. She came to Washington on a shopping trip—or that's what she told Howard. Susan liked jewelry and liked being photographed. What do you want me to say? Don't you have some sexual quirk? Do you like to hand-cuff your wife or pistol-whip your girlfriend?"

"None of my girlfriends ever ended up dead in a canal, Congressman," Harter replied. "She was wearing this jewelry when she was found."

"Look," said Canley, "I don't have to murder someone to get what I want."

"I haven't accused you of anything," said Harter.

"How can I explain to you about Susan and me? I'd been widowed for a year, and my wife had been ill for a long time. Howard hadn't exactly been captivating Susan lately. We sparked something in each other. That's all."

"You didn't see her Thursday, the night she turned up missing?"

"I wish I had. Things might have been different. She might not have driven to that alley. She might still be alive. She was upset with me. I'd called her in the afternoon and told her I didn't see how we could get together. I had to go to a dinner with some religious leaders and then on to a rally with some businessmen. She was very insistent about needing to see me. She reminded me how she'd sneaked around all summer, even taking off work on afternoons I was in town. She claimed I never changed my schedule for her. I told her I'd call her about ten if I could get away. I couldn't. After the business group, some party people cornered me and had me sit in on a strategy session till after midnight. The next morning I went back to Washington. At that point I didn't know anything had happened to her. You're trying to make me out the heavy, but Susan and I were lovers. Don't you understand?"

Harter stayed silent as he absorbed what Canley had told him. Nothing conflicted in any way with what Jack Reese or anybody else had said. Susan Devendall quite possibly had driven to the alley alone that night, frustrated by not being able to get her photos from Reese earlier in the evening, frustrated by not being able to see Canley because, for him, politicking came first. But what had happened in the alley?

"Did you ever hear of a Daniel Jones or a Simon Bowman?" he asked Canley.

"No. Should I have?"

"Susan Devendall never mentioned either of them?"

"The names mean nothing."

Harter stared at Canley's face a moment. The congressman was looking out the second-story window and, this time, Harter could only see his photogenic right profile. He began shoving the jewelry back in the envelope.

"I meant what I said, Harter," snapped Canley, turning full-face toward him. "I told you I'd level. I answered every one of your questions. If any of this shit ever comes back to haunt me, I'll bust your ass."

··· 25 ···

Harter stuffed his cigarette butt in the sand of the concrete ashtray outside the courthouse door and went down the steps to his car. He unlocked it, took one photo out of an envelope, left the rest of the evidence inside, then locked up again. With the picture in his hand, he began walking toward Howard P. Devendall's office.

It was a sunny October day fit for making his rounds on foot. He'd hiked about two blocks from the courthouse when he saw her come out of the building. A gray-uniformed black driver opened the limousine door for the short lady in the violet coat.

Harter cut across the street, through the late morning traffic, and reached the limo right after the chauffeur had climbed in. He rapped at her window. Amy Devendall said something to her driver and the window powered down.

"Downtown on business, Mrs. Devendall?" asked Harter, catching a whiff of her strong perfume.

"Howard wanted me to sign some papers," she answered. "Then we looked over some of our buildings. My husband bought this entire block just after World War Two, shortly before he died. We've been thinking about remodeling some of it, but decided to wait to see what happens with the downtown.

Perhaps some condominiums might be a good idea, don't you think, Detective?"

"I wouldn't know." Sensing she wasn't about to bring up the case, Harter went at her another way. "I've been running into a few people who know you."

"Yes? Who?"

"A Reverend Sam Knotts, for instance."

"Sam's really a client of Howard's," she said, turning her rouged cheek away from him in disinterest. "How did you happen to meet him?"

"Well, you know, this case has two parts. It's not just the murder of your daughter-in-law. An old man died in an arson, too. I've learned another old man died under similar circumstances in August. Sam Knotts was his minister."

"You've lost me, Detective."

"It might not be important, but did your daughter-in-law ever talk about either Simon Bowman or Daniel Jones?"

"I don't believe I ever heard of them." To emphasize her point, she stared directly at him. "I'll ask Howard about them, if it would help."

Harter glanced over at the building. "You don't have to. I may go in and see him myself."

"He's terribly busy. He couldn't even take time to go to Maxi's with me for lunch."

Maxi's, he thought, the place where Susan Devendall had told Ace Stewart he could get a job as a dishwasher.

"I won't take much of your son's time," said Harter. "I thought he might like to know Congressman Canley will be attending the memorial service tomorrow. I just spent most of the morning with the congressman."

"Yes, and what did Charles have to say for himself?" Amy Devendall asked in a detached manner that couldn't quite cover her curiousity.

"He's upset. Says he didn't know there was anything wrong when he left Shawnee early last Friday morning."

"No one knew there was anything wrong last Friday morning," she said. "I'm sure Howard will be glad to know Charles will be at the service. It's so nice to have friends around on such occasions."

"Are they old friends, your son and Congressman Canley?"

"They've been friends and associates in the past," she responded in a voice that showed she knew what Harter was after. "Of course, you know how associations change, Detective."

"Has anything come to mind since Tuesday, anything that might throw some light on what happened to your daughter-in-law?"

"Nothing I can think of," she said. "Now, if you don't mind, I have a luncheon engagement."

Harter backed away from the limousine, the window powered up, and the car pulled away from the curb. He rested against the parking meter a moment to collect his thoughts before going into the building.

Howard Devendall's secretary gave him the once-over when he stepped through the office door. At first she told him Mr. Devendall was in conference and couldn't be interrupted. But when he flashed his badge and mentioned the murder investigation, she hurried into the inner office. Soon she was back to usher him inside.

Devendall was seated behind an enormous polished desk. Despite the piles of legal documents and law books, there was something extremely tidy about the place. Howard, in his white shirt and gray vest, looked tidy as well. Harter felt like a hippie at a White House ball.

"I don't have much time, Detective," said Devendall. "I've been trying to catch up on my backlog."

"Just a couple questions." He handed the lawyer Reese's photo of the sign at the cardboard box factory. "How long have you owned the building by the canal?"

"We've owned it from the start. It was one of my father's first projects. He built it about 1910, when he was still a young man. We've leased it to a series of industries over the years. I believe it was a tannery originally."

"It's totally empty now?"

"As far as I'm aware. Why are you asking?"

"Would you mind if I looked through it?"

"I don't understand."

"You do realize your wife's body was found not far from the building, and that we believe she was held captive someplace for a day or so?"

Devendall's face became paler than usual. "I guess I didn't make the connection. Certainly you don't think—"

"I don't think anything. I'd just like to look at the building."

Devendall leaned forward and hit an intercom button. "Mrs. Jackson, would you find a master key for the cardboard box factory and give it to Detective Harter when he leaves?"

"Thanks. It'll save a lot of time."

"I told you the other day, I'll help in any way I can to find my wife's murderer. Anything else?"

"Daniel Jones or Simon Bowman? Did your wife ever bring up those names? She may have met them when she worked for the Commission on Aging."

"Truth is, the only time we talked about her work was when I'd encourage her to quit. I didn't pay attention to the names of her clients. Again, I don't understand what they'd have to do with it. Now the man who tried to rape her—that might be something else."

"I've seen him," said Harter. "I don't consider him a suspect at this time."

"Whom *do* you consider a suspect, Detective?" asked Devendall, gripping the arms of his chair.

"I've nothing to say publicly," answered Harter, rising and stepping toward the door. "I'll get the key back to you early next week."

"Did"—Devendall stopped and then started again—"Did you ever find out about the jewelry?"

"Your wife got it at a craft fair in Washington."

"That doesn't help your case much, does it?"

"No." Harter continued toward the door. Just before leaving, he said, "By the way, I spoke with Congressman Canley this morning. He sends his sympathy. He says he'll be at the service tomorrow."

"You won't be, will you?" asked Howard Devendall.

"I hadn't thought about it," said Harter.

Later, sitting at the counter at the Desert Island, Harter wondered if there was any reason he *should* attend the service. Detectives always did that in the movies, but he never had. He also wondered if telling Devendall about Canley had been too low a blow.

He shook off the thought. He was trying to solve a murder, not make friends.

Two murders actually.

Maybe even three.

Everyone forgot that.

He studied the waitress' face as she slid the plate of hot dogs in front of him. He noticed that her heavy makeup was serving a purpose, swooping across her cheekbones and covering a right eye that was still bruised and a left eye that looked like it was just returning to normal.

Do you like to handcuff your wife or pistol-whip your girlfriend? A weird line coming from a congressman.

Don't you have some sexual quirk? Was Canley sending a message or mounting a defense?

From all the evidence, Susan Devendall had had unexpected sides to her personality.

What had Linda Dean said? *It was like she had a split personality.* The air-conditioned Volkswagen. The clothes buyer who wore jeans and an old raincoat to work. The woman who didn't confide in other women, yet was willing to bare herself to a total stranger's camera. Possessor of a streak of social consciousness that had dissolved enough to allow her to become entangled with the most conservative of congressmen. Resident of a westside mansion, but found dead in suggestive attire in Shantytown after being slugged around, no more protected than the waitress with the black eyes.

Ace Stewart could be telling the truth. She could have come on to him, then backed off screaming in fear. Within a month of that incident, she was inching away from social work and falling into siestas with Canley.

Harter hated such psychologizing. Yet he had to admit that fathoming Susan Devendall appeared to require a wall of degrees.

Still, when all the psychologizing was over, the two old men remained.

The dead old men from Wild Stream, West Virginia.

··· 26 ···

As soon as he crossed the river bridge, the road veered to the right through a relatively flat valley, the mountains rolling down to a nearly farmable level. The woods were autumn-thin and colored leaves dried in piles along the narrow state road.

Harter's eyes were as stuck to the road as his mind was on Liz. She'd tried to talk her way into joining him on the West Virginia trip, and he hadn't let her.

He'd laid out his plan Friday night, and she'd taken it so badly that he'd intended to slip away without waking her Saturday morning. But, as he sat on the edge of her bed putting on his shoes, her voice had broken through the early morning stillness.

"I could still put a sign on the door and go with you. We could make a weekend of it."

"Hell, you sound like Caruthers. He came in yesterday when I was calling the Wild Stream police chief and wanted to know where I was headed. Rather than tell him, I asked him how you write off champagne on police-department vouchers. He got pretty grouchy. Told me I'd get mine one day."

"I'll pay for the champagne," she'd said. "Remember, tonight was to be your birthday dinner."

He'd looked over his shoulder at her, at her gray-green eyes staring his way, at her dark hair against the pillow, at her tanned face with the covers pulled up around it.

"I just want to get there and get back. I don't even know if it's worth driving down there. I'm not really looking forward to it."

"You know you are. You'll enjoy it. You can complain about your job all you like, but it's the only thing that grabs you, the only thing that keeps you going."

"You grab me."

"Sometimes I wonder."

"I wouldn't have stayed around this long if you didn't. It's not like I have to."

"Are you positive you'll be back tonight?" she'd asked.

"I'm not positive of anything. I'll call you when I have an idea. I may be late."

"I'll wait until midnight and then everything will turn back into a pumpkin, mice, and rags."

He'd leaned over and kissed her. "I hope I'll at least find the glass slipper."

He'd put on his gun and jacket and gone out into the brisk morning air. Liz's neighborhood had been quiet at 7:30. He'd climbed into his car, driven out of the west side, over the bridge, and headed south.

Near the South Shawnee rail yards, he'd stopped for coffee and doughts at a diner that always reminded him of the Edward Hopper print on his wall. The joint had been around longer than he had. His father had once had a regular stool in the place.

Crossing the Shawnee city line, he'd driven past a string of fast-food restaurants, a shopping center, the Reverend Sam Knotts' True Church of God with its Christian Academy-to-be. Then, passing the road to the Hays Trailer Court and salvage yard, he'd finally found himself on open highway between two mountain ridges.

"So the city boy will be going to the country?" Liz had lightly taunted him the evening before when he'd told her what he was about to do. He supposed he'd never told her how well he knew those mountains south of town. How many times over the years had he retreated up the north slope to the overlook and surveyed the city below him? But he'd never taken her with him.

When he'd been young, the west slope of South Mountain, above the city reservoir, had been his father's favorite camping spot. They'd pitch a tent in the old CCC camp, where his dad had worked during the Depression. Out there on the mountain, they'd haul water from an old hand pump and rough it for days. He'd wandered that hillside, every inch, just as he would later wander the city at all hours.

Someday he'd have to take Liz out on the mountain to see if anything remained of the CCC camp and that other world.

The road turned away from the mountain. To his right now, the Shawnee–Potomac mainline cut through a hollow and, two tracks wide, began to parallel the highway. He knew he'd be following the railroad, or the railroad would be following him, all the way to Wild Stream. The mainline ran its way south, then west, deep into West Virginia, the Mountain State, down past the coal mines, coal camps, those old company towns where his mother's mother had been born.

His grandmother had had incredible stories of the coal fields, of the kind of strike warfare that history classes ignored. Maybe he'd dress as his coal-mining great-grandfather for the Halloween Party.

The night before, Liz had again reminded him of the party the next weekend at the Winhams. She had known he didn't want to go. "What do you think you'll wear as a costume?" she'd asked, as if the debate was more over what to go as than over whether to go at all.

If he went, he'd decided, he'd rub black diamonds over his face and on the soles of his boots so they'd leave footprints on the carpet.

Coalminer blackface.

She'd hate it.

So many distances between them.

Amazing that they could sometimes reach out to one another that far.

He was racing to overcome a diesel pulling empty coal cars when the Wild Stream sign came up on him. He hit his brakes and slowed down. The freight swung off to the right, the engineer still gunning it, building steam for the mountain back of town.

Wild Stream was a small burg set for the most part in a valley, though frame cubicles rose up the hillsides around him. He hoped he was wrong, but he feared the visit might end up as clueless as his Friday afternoon tour through the abandoned cardboard box factory on the canal bank. There had been nothing inside, no signs of anyone being kept there, no recent garbage, no chains. Unless the company continued to make long-term lease payments, the Devendall family certainly wasn't bringing in much income from the dingy building.

When he reached the traffic light by the two-story brick courthouse—the largest structure in town—Harter remembered the police chief's directions and pulled into the first parking place he came to. Looking back, he saw he'd already sailed past The Diamond.

Outside, the restaurant was painted bright blue, with plenty of glass, making it the liveliest-looking spot on Main Street.

Inside, the formica tabletops sparkled. The wooden booths and the elaborate soda fountain mirror hinted that the eatery was well-established and, once, might have deserved its reputation.

Harter headed straight to the squat man with a crew cut who was sitting at the counter playing with a coffee spoon as he chatted with a waitress. "You Ben Lynch?"

The man tilted toward him so he could see his white shirt and the badge beneath his dark jacket. "Yeah."

"I'm Edward Harter from the Shawnee police."

"You don't look much like a detective," said Lynch in the kind of relaxed country voice that a city cop couldn't keep long.

"If you let me be a detective, I'll let you be a police chief," Harter said back.

Lynch cracked a grin. "Sit down. Bertie, bring this man a cup of coffee. The good stuff. From yesterday." After Harter had climbed on a stool, Lynch asked, "Any trouble getting here?"

"No. Nice drive. Gave me time to think. You got anyone lined up for us to see?"

Lynch reached into his pocket and pulled out a small notepad as Bertie put a cup of black liquid in front of Harter.

"After we talked yesterday, I made a list of a few old-timers that may know something of Bowman and Jones," said Lynch.

"Great. How about old police files? You didn't find anything, did you?"

Lynch shook his head. "I had one of my girls look through things quick. She didn't turn up nothing. That's not to say there couldn't be something in circuit court records or someplace. The old records are pretty incomplete. Nobody required half the paperwork they load us down with now."

"The good old days, huh?"

"Must have been. I'm still not clear on precisely what these old fellows have to do with your case."

Harter slowly worked at the coffee as he explained what he knew to Ben Lynch—the arson, Susan Devendall, the Commission on Aging files, how both Bowman and Jones had been born in Wild Stream, how his trip was just a long shot. He held back on Charles Whitford Canley and a few things he didn't figure the police chief needed to know.

When he'd told the tale, Lynch nodded his bristly head and tossed a dollar bill on the counter. "You ready to get going?"

"Sure."

"We'll take my car. It'll be simpler," said Lynch. He led the way out of The Diamond, down the sidewalk half a block, and stopped beside a late-model white vehicle with WILD STREAM POLICE DEPARTMENT and a town seal stenciled on the door.

"We'll start with the boys right in town," said Lynch, pulling away from the curb. "This first one's a real old-timer. Ken Carlson's in his upper eighties. Lived around here all his life. He can be a trifle senile, I'll warn you. Some days he's sharp, others he's not."

Soon Lynch was turning the car into a driveway that curved away from Main Street and up a hill.

An hour later, as they drove back out the driveway, Harter was beginning to worry about having wasted a day.

This Saturday had not been one of Ken Carlson's more lucid ones.

He'd started out well enough: "Daniel Jones and Simon Bowman? Sure I recall them. They was in school with me. Don't know whether they finished or not."

Then Carlson had gone off on a rambling description of the one-room schoolhouse, the teachers, their chastising paddle, even the weather one January day when the kids had had to hike through snowdrifts—"not like these spoiled young ones today."

After that, there was no getting him back on track.

Lynch's second old-timer wasn't much better. Nor was the third, or the fourth. After considerable driving around, a stop back at The Diamond for lunch, and four hours of interviews, they'd learned little.

Whether or not they'd finished school, Daniel Jones and Simon Bowman had both served in France during World War I. When they'd come home in 1919, it was the old singsong—"How you gonna keep them down in Wild Stream?" They'd earned reputations for carousing and womanizing. Low-paying day jobs around town didn't suit them. Eventually they'd headed to Shawnee, which must have seemed like the Promised Land. After that, no one knew anything.

"Ain't coming together, is it?" asked Lynch as he drove east of Wild Stream, past a small market.

"No, it ain't coming together. Look, I appreciate everything you've done, but unless this next one knows something, I'll be heading back to Shawnee," said Harter. At least he could salvage the evening with Liz.

"Well, if Jerome don't know nothing, that's probably the wisest thing to do," said Lynch, turning off onto a rutted lane. "Jerome Ball's more or less the local historian. I saved the best for last."

Crossing the yard to the frame farmhouse, Harter hoped Jerome Ball would be forthright with them, that if he had nothing to say worth saying, he'd tell them right off and be done with it.

Turned out Ball had a lot worth saying, and he did say it right off.

"Simon Bowman was a real bastard," Ball proclaimed as he moved around the kitchen, making them coffee and bacon-and-tomato sandwiches on a cast-iron stove. "I was about ten when he came home from the war—World War One. My daddy hired him now and then to do odd jobs, so I saw a good bit of him.

Even as a full-grown man, he'd throw stones at birds."

"And Daniel Jones?" asked Harter.

"Daniel was a whole other piece of cake. Nice fellow, fairly smart. You'd never have imagined the pair would be best friends, inseparable. It was like Daniel never saw just how mean Simon could be. They must have left here about 1923—I guess I was fourteen or so. They were expecting to get jobs with the railroad in Shawnee. I heard bits and pieces about it later. When Daniel would come back to town, like he would occasionally, I'd ask him about Simon and Amelia Logan."

"Amelia Logan?"

"She ran off to Shawnee with them. I'd judge she was sixteen at the time." The lines on Ball's thin face twisted into a lopsided grin. "Amelia'd been running a regular screwing business since she was thirteen or fourteen. Her mother either didn't know or didn't care. She was usually off with some man, anyway. God knows where her daddy was. They pictured themselves as what you'd call fallen elite. Traced the decline to being on the wrong side in the Civil War."

"Screwing business?" asked Ben Lynch. "You mean Amelia Logan was a whore?"

"Yeah. Story went that Amelia had a code for telling her customers if it was all right for them to come in. If she was alone and open for business, she'd hang a silk stocking on the clothesline beside the house. It's where the water plant is now." Lynch nodded. "The customer was supposed to collect the silk stocking from the line and bring it to the door so's no one else would come. They say Amelia had all the men in town around her finger. Or around her thigh."

"And she went to Shawnee with Jones and Bowman, and you never heard of her again?" asked Harter.

"Right," said Jerome Ball, leaning forward on his elbows on the kitchen table. "When I'd ask Daniel about her or Simon, he'd just grimace. No one around here lost sleep over any of them, though I kind of missed Daniel. I'm sure, with all her enterprise, Amelia took care of herself pretty well—at least as long as her looks held out. She *was* a good-looker. She probably earned herself a whole batch of stuff monogrammed A.L."

"A.L.," mumbled Harter, putting down his sandwich.

"Amelia Logan—that'd be her initials," explained Ball, as if the detective might have missed something.

··· 27 ···

His left hand resting on her smooth thigh, his knees pressed against the back of hers, he laid still, watching the room slowly lighten.

She knew nothing of what he'd picked up in Wild Stream. When he'd arrived at her studio shortly before nine, she'd already had the wine uncorked and the table ready. They'd banished all serious talk.

Three glasses of wine later, the dishes piled in the sink, the stereo playing saxophone ballads, he had reached out to her, across the great distance, urging her toward him, undoing the top button of her black dress, sliding a hand to her breasts, rubbing gently at her knee. Women were so different.

They'd begun the slow garment-by-garment stripping of each other, the stripping away of cloth and of psychological layers, reducing the gap between them until, he inside her, she around him, there was no gap, for the moment, and he could forget his name was Edward Harter, forget he was a cop, and just roll with her, roll with her, with her.

He awoke near dawn but tried not to move, holding her instead, taking in the feel of her, staying close so the distance wouldn't widen.

His body safe and secure for the moment, his mind reviewed

events of the last few days. It had only been a week since the chief had called him away from Liz to the canal bank on that dreary Saturday night. All those facts, conjectures, old tales that he'd come across since had been unknown to him only seven days before.

Susan Devendall, Daniel Jones, Simon Bowman, Jack Reese, Tattoo Kendall, Amy Devendall, Howard P., Canley, Knotts, Amelia Logan . . . all those people he was starting to know well, too well, had been strangers a short while before.

All those bricks . . . and yet he still couldn't put the building together. He had to pick up one of them and throw it and see how far it went and what, or who, it hit. He knew that. But which one?

He had to get moving.

He carefully disengaged himself from Liz and, trying not to disturb her, climbed out of bed, scooped up his clothes, and went into the bathroom. He was aware the shower might wake her, but he needed one and took the chance. When he returned to her bedroom, she was sitting up.

"Working today?" she asked as soon as she saw he was dressed.

"Yeah."

"Is it getting close?"

"Yeah."

"Call me."

"I will."

He bent over, kissed her, and then, as he had the morning before, went out to his car and drove south.

He got to Sam Knotts' True Church of God as the last churchgoers were hurrying into the white building for the nine o'clock service. He pulled onto the berm on the other side of the highway and stared at the church, then lit a cigarette and rolled down his window. Inside, faint voices rose in a hymn.

Soon the Reverend Knotts would be preaching. He might stand high in his pulpit, mouthing a silent sermon, waving an arm that ended in a bloody stub.

Christ.

He'd pondered Ace Stewart's words several times since Wednesday. *If I lie, cut off my dick. Ain't that what they used to do? Like robbers, they cut off their hands, and liars they cut out their tongues, and rapists they cut off their dicks.*

If those ancient laws were ever enforced, thought Harter, imagine all the maimed people in pulpits, in the halls of Congress, in houses, in the streets.

His right hand slid across his black jacket until he felt his gun.

A van came down the highway, pulled into the church lot, and parked near the Christian Academy sign. *Made possible by friends of The True Church of God and by a donation In Memory of A.L.*

The van door slid open and a gang of kids poured out and headed around the side of the church to the Sunday school rooms.

Raise up the children right, Knotts had said to him as he'd crowded him on the orange sofa.

Harter leaned back and tapped out a rhythm on the steering wheel.

How the hell was he going to get at Knotts?

He couldn't prove anything yet.

The key—if there was one—was A.L.

He turned the key in the ignition, U-turned back toward Shawnee, and stopped at the diner near the railroad shops to call the chief—to disturb *his* tranquil Sunday morning for once.

Leaving the diner, he drove crosstown, up the Avenue, onto Thomas Street, and into Baxter Street. He halted a minute behind Reese's house to scout out the location. Then he headed back down the alley, past the piled char of Daniel Jones' house, around the block and up Thomas Street once more, all the way to the top of the hill, where he turned around and drove back down, pulling up to the curb across from the brick house.

Lighting another cigarette, he surveyed the steep street and the layout of the two-family house. Convincing himself that the plan would work was actually harder than convincing the chief. Harter didn't want anyone to get hurt, didn't want the house destroyed if things got out of hand.

He watched a short heavyset woman leave the house and go down the hill. Mrs. Kendall. On her way to church, he guessed. Good. Better to talk to Tattoo alone.

He climbed out of the car, crossed Thomas Street and knocked on the door. He was a little surprised when Jack Reese answered.

Reese stared at him awkwardly for a moment, then motioned him in. "How you doing? Back to see Tattoo again?"

"Yeah, we were running through some ancient history when I stopped in Thursday afternoon. I wanted to go over some of the ground again. How are you doing?"

"Better."

"Your dreams improving?"

"Improving," said Reese as he moved to the head of the kitchen steps and called for Tattoo.

The photographer walked back to the couch and cleared away sections of Sunday's *Pittsburgh Press*. "Sit down. Are you still tracking the Bowman guy?"

Harter nodded.

"Anything new on the case?"

"Stop worrying," said Harter.

Tattoo's slow, heavy footsteps got nearer. He had a chaw of tobacco in his jaw when he entered the living room. "You again," he said.

"Me again."

Tattoo dropped into his chair. "What can I do for you?"

Glancing across the sofa at Jack Reese, Harter decided it was safe to talk. Reese might even be an asset. "I just wondered if you'd remembered anything more that Daniel Jones said about Simon Bowman."

"I been thinking on that name, Simon Bowman," said Tattoo. "I talked to a couple old boys about it. Ain't much new. I can't recall Daniel ever saying nothing about a Bowman at any length, but somewheres it does mean something. I got it in my head Bowman was a scab, like I told you the other day. Maybe more than that, some of the old boys think."

"Like what?"

"Like, could be this Simon Bowman was a company thug or some such thing back in 'twenty-eight or 'thirty-four, or one of them mean strikes in them days. The name's got an evil ring to me. Could be that Daniel or old Jack—that'd be Jack here's granddaddy—mentioned him years ago. You know how these things are. The stories all blend together after a time, particularly when you got no reason to memorize them and you don't know the people they're about. Anyways, the bosses in them days would hire blackshirts, real criminal sorts. For all I know, the governor'd let felons out of the pen to be strikebreakers and head-bashing guards. I just wish the young ones could remember them days. There is one thing, though."

"What?"

"Devendall. Wasn't that the name? Wasn't that the dead girl's name?"

"Yeah," said Harter. He could feel Reese tense next to him.

Tattoo shot brown juice into his spittoon. "Some of the boys say a Devendall was who contracted thugs for the railroad. He used to scour Shantytown for real tough ones. His name was probably James Howard Devendall. 'Course he'd be long gone now, wouldn't he? He wouldn't have been a young man even then."

"His wife's still around," said Harter. "Susan Devendall was married to his son."

"The old lady must be quite an antique."

"I'd judge she was considerably younger than James Howard Devendall when they married," answered Harter, recalling Howard had said his father had built the box factory in 1910.

"What's it mean?" asked Reese.

"I don't know." Harter looked back at Tattoo. "Did you ever hear of an Amelia Logan? She might have come from Wild Stream, West Virginia, along with Simon Bowman or Daniel Jones."

"Don't mean nothing to me. I can't seem to dredge more up out of my head right now. I wish I could, but I can't."

"You've done fine."

Tattoo shook his head. "I wish I could help you more. I want to nail the bastard that burnt up Daniel and killed the girl."

"So do I," said Reese.

Harter leaned back against the afghan spread over the daybed. He lit a cigarette and, from the corner of his eye, caught Reese's sad expression. He wondered how Reese would react to the news that the best aid he could give would be to go away and leave his house empty for a few days.

Then he stared at the old man in the faded flannel shirt with the left sleeve pinned up. Was he ready for the danger?

After a long pause, Harter came out with it.

"There is a way you can both help."

··· 28 ···

"I live on Thomas Street, right above the alley where Daniel Jones' house was," explained Tattoo. "You'd best come see me. Daniel told me everything before the fire."

Harter, his hand over the mouthpiece of another phone, listened to the fumbling response. Sitting at his desk, Caruthers watched the old railroader and the younger detective closely, his expression betraying his doubt that the scheme would work.

"Yeah. He told me everything. All about the old days," insisted Tattoo. "All about Simon Bowman and Amelia Logan."

He was doing a fantastic job, thought Harter. He was sticking tight to the script, setting things up perfectly. Harter hoped he'd done his own scene-setting properly. He hoped they'd called the right person. But he wouldn't have bet his life on it.

"That's the name. Tattoo Kendall. I told you the address already. You'll find it. You never had no trouble finding Daniel or Bowman, did you? But I'll be ready for you. Don't try nothing on me. Just bring money. Make my retirement a load easier. I'll be alone tonight and Monday night. Don't come in the day. If you don't show, I'm sure a lot of people, like the police, would like to hear what I got to say."

The voice at the other end mildly pleaded ignorance, or innocence, of what he was talking about. Harter nodded for him to cut off the conversation.

"I ain't got time for this. You come see me face-to-face and talk it out," said Tattoo before slamming down the phone.

Harter listened and imagined he heard a long sigh before the click and the dial tone.

Hanging up, he said to the old man, "You should have been an actor."

"What if nothing comes of it?" Caruthers asked Harter.

"Then I made the wrong choice."

"Not the first time."

"You got a better idea?" asked Tattoo, instinctively siding with Harter.

"Him?" said Harter. "He's got no idea."

"So I'm cautious," said Caruthers. "I'm not into this game-playing."

"Come on. It's already dark. We've got to get going," said Harter, having no heart for a debate on moderation. "You do know what you're supposed to do, Caruthers?"

"Yeah. You're lucky the chief called me up personally."

"You got more important things to do tonight?" asked Harter. When Caruthers didn't answer, he pushed in another spur. "You better get something to eat before you go on stakeout. It's bound to be a long night. Mattioni's is just down the street. Open Sunday evenings. I'll vouch for the place. Full line of hoagies—and *no meatloaf.*"

Caruthers ignored him and hurried out of the room as Harter lit a cigarette. He'd already driven away by the time the other two left headquarters.

"Your partner ain't got much faith in your plan," said Tattoo, climbing into the car.

"Ah, he's like that. No imagination. Wants everything

wrapped up neat. Caruthers isn't exactly my partner. He'll do his job, though. He's competent. He's a cop despite the complaining."

He steered out onto the empty Sunday-night street.

"So now we just wait?" asked Tattoo.

"Yeah, we just wait—and stay sharp. I warned you this could be dangerous."

"I made it through World War Two and plenty of other bad scenes," said Tattoo, rubbing at his stub.

Later I'll ask him. There'll be lots of time later. Harter crossed the tracks into the east side.

"How many cops you going to have planted around?" asked Tattoo.

"Three, besides Caruthers and me. The chief told me to pick who I wanted. I've got three beat cops lined up, guys who've done a good job with me over the years. Guys who'd like to be detectives. Guys who want my job, or Caruthers'."

"What if Caruthers is right? What if it don't work? What if we called the wrong person?"

Harter said nothing, and drove up the hill in silence. He didn't want to face up to that possibility.

When he reached Baxter Street, he turned the corner and drove on until he was behind Tattoo's house. Stopping, he said, "You go on in. I'll get rid of this car, check on the other guys, and be with you in a few minutes."

Tattoo opened the door with his right hand and climbed out. Then Harter continued down the alley until he spotted the unmarked vehicle with the three cops inside. He parked in front of them and, after looking around to be sure no one was watching, got out of his car and climbed in with them.

The cops in the smoky Chevy were dressed in grubby plainclothes, dark enough to blend into the chilly night. Harter carefully went over the plan with them again.

Everyone was to have a hand-held radio and report to him on suspicious people or vehicles in the neighborhood.

Clark was to give him ten minutes to get into Tattoo's house before making his own way up to Jack Reese's kitchen and stationing himself by the back-door window. Harter handed him a key that Reese had provided a few hours earlier.

Ten minutes after Clark left the car, McManaway was to head up the alley and seat himself in Reese's old Ford for the night.

Bettles was to stay with the vehicle, ready to drive wherever directed.

Harter opened the door and began walking slowly up the alley as if he were out for an evening stroll. With a radio stuffed inside his jacket, he checked out the buildings on the hillside above him, noting what lights were lit on Thomas Street.

What if he was wrong? What if it didn't work? he asked himself.

Perhaps he had rushed it. Perhaps he should have spent a couple more days on the investigation before going for the kill. He was still learning things, like the fact that old Devendall might have hired thugs. There was so much he didn't know, though he'd never have admitted it to Caruthers.

Four pork chops were sizzling in a black skillet when Harter stepped into the kitchen. Tattoo was standing at the table with a giant butcher knife in his hand, awkwardly chopping a mammoth potato. When he was through wielding the knife, he dropped the potato slices in the skillet to fry along with the chops.

"I been meaning to ask you," said Tattoo as he turned the homefries with a metal spatula. "You ain't Bill Harter's son, are you?"

"You knew my father?"

"Not too good, just knowed who he was. So you grew up on his side of town?"

"East Shawnee, born and bred."

All through supper, Tattoo kept up the chatter about Bill Harter, the railroad neighborhoods, the Shawnee–Potomac. Now and then, when it wasn't too obvious, Harter studied the old man. Tattoo was finding it hard to cut his chop one-handed and finally picked it up and gnawed on the bone.

Later.

They were washing the dishes when the first radio report came in.

"Same blue van's been up and down the hill several times," said Caruthers. "Looks like it's turning into the alley."

"Coming this way slow," said McManaway. "It's passing. Looks like teenagers."

"It's going on down," piped in Bettles a minute later.

"Probably kids looking for a place to park and party," Harter said to Tattoo. "In my days, we used to go out to the overlook on the mountain."

"I guess they stopped calling that Lover's Leap. That's always been a prime parking spot. Used to be filled with Model T's on Saturday night when I first come to Shawnee. I bet that woman you was asking about seen her share of Lover's Leap."

"Amelia Logan?"

"Yeah, that one." He smiled.

Later.

Around nine o'clock, Harter went up to the dark third floor and peeped out a front window. Across the street, slightly up the hill, sat Caruthers' car. Moving to a back window, he had much the same view of the alley as Clark would. A streetlight reflected off the top of Reese's Ford. He hoped McManaway couldn't be seen inside.

Looking down the hill, beyond the metal garages in the alley, ~e could see the lights of cars speeding up the Avenue toward

his old neighborhood. Below the Avenue, a freight cut through town.

When he went back downstairs, Tattoo was sitting in his overstuffed chair in the living room, putting a load of tobacco in his mouth. The blinds were shut and the curtains pulled closed.

"You do what you want. Watch TV or whatever," Harter told him. "I'll be in your back room so I don't have to move if anyone comes."

He walked to the next room and positioned himself in a soft chair in the dark parlor—the room where, on the other side of the house, Reese had set up his studio.

He waited.

"How late does this thing go on?" called Tattoo.

"We'll be here all night and all tomorrow night. If nobody comes by, say, one o'clock, you can go to bed if you want," Harter called back.

"You know, I already miss May. We ain't slept apart but a handful of times since we was married."

"Well, she's safer at the motel. I'll see you get out there tomorrow to visit her for a few hours. That way you won't be around here."

"There's a car . . ." Caruthers began. "Forget it."

"You asked me about my father—now let me ask you something I've wondered," said Harter.

"Shoot," returned Tattoo's voice.

"I'd be interested in knowing how you lost your arm."

"It was in . . . I was in . . . the wrong place at the wrong time, like they say."

"Where was that?" pressed Harter. It was easier to ask such questions when you weren't looking at the person, when you were in a separate room and the other person was only a voice.

"Wasn't in the war or nothing so dramatic. No Devendall

thug, no Simon Bowman beat on me in a strike. Somehow I got in between two refrigerator cars a-coupling one night. I don't remember much else. I passed out from the pain and woke up in the hospital, the arm gone. Lucky I lived, I suppose. I knew a man died like that. Boxcars went together with him right between them. I heard him screaming myself. When they pulled the front car away, he crumpled to the tracks, almost in two halves, blood all over. Some people think it's weird these things happen. People think you're crazy or something, not being able to hear the trains and all. But when you live and work around them, you start to ignore the noise, or you don't hear it. Then you're caught one day."

"I know," said Harter when the voice in the other room had settled into a pause. "I had an uncle—my grandmother's brother—who got hit by a coal train and was killed years ago. Just walked right in front of it."

"Well, I lived. Armless, but I lived. Weird thing is, sometimes I feel like I got a left arm. Feels like I can flex the muscle and see the girl slink, the girl in the tattoo I used to have. But when I try, there's nothing there. Two refrigerator cars coupling one night, that's all. How'd your father die?"

Harter didn't respond for a long while. He was relieved when Bettles' voice cut in: "Man walking up the alley your way. Bag in his hand."

A minute later, McManaway reported, "I see him. Bottle in the bag. He's got an old Army jacket on. Wino going on by."

"Hasn't even been a car down the hill in almost fifteen minutes," added Caruthers.

What if it didn't work?

"You made my left arm itch and there's nothing to scratch," said Tattoo. "The itch says nothing's going to happen tonight."

A moment later, the sound of the television hit the air. Harter listened to the headlines. Sunday night, and they were still showing film of Congressman Canley's Friday press conference. Must have been a slow weekend.

"Son of a bitch," he heard Tattoo say.

"Son of a bitch," he agreed.

As the weather and sports droned on, Harter wished he was with Liz, just as he knew Tattoo wished he was with May.

There's nothing to scratch.

He wanted a cigarette but he didn't want the smoke in the room.

New thought for the costume party: put a shirt on over his left arm and tie up the sleeve.

··· 29 ···

"Getting damn cold out here," grouched Caruthers on Monday night.

"Turn on your heater," Harter radioed back, trying to sound just as irritated.

Sooner or later, he knew, he would have to face up to it.

"Nice and toasty in here," came Clark's voice from Reese's kitchen. "I've got a pot of coffee on."

"Can't complain," said McManaway. "I got the front seat pushed back and a luscious blonde sitting bare-assed on my lap. Hope we're here all night."

Tense as he was, Harter almost laughed. Dave McManaway had always been his choice to replace Caruthers.

Of course, *he* might be the one who got replaced, busted down to the rank of street cop if his plan failed.

What if nothing happened?

At best, the chief would shoot him a nasty frown and grumble about his department budget not being geared to have five cops tied up doing nothing for two nights.

Caruthers would never let him forget it. He'd spread the tale around the force. Clark, Bettles, and McManaway would get in their digs whenever they saw him coming.

All that was the easy part.

He'd also have to arrange further protection for Tattoo and May for a week or so in case the bloody arsonist showed up late. Worse still, if he stayed on the case, he'd have to go at it from a whole new angle, hoping his ploy hadn't scared off his suspects.

Maybe he had miscalculated. The plan had hit him like a bullet while he'd sat in front of The True Church of God on Sunday morning. He'd gone all the way with it, uncritically. Maybe they had called the wrong person.

"Now to recap the news," said the WBRT anchorman. "A Bartlesburg couple died tonight when their pickup truck stalled on the James Road railroad crossing and was struck by a train. Knobtown High's football team has a shot at going through the season undefeated. And, with a little more than a week until election day, the local political scene is heating up."

Harter sat in the dark parlor, half-listening to a series of commercials until a voice announced that the late show starred Jane Russell, but he missed the name of it. It didn't matter. Then he heard a jar lid being unscrewed and the crinkle of waxpaper.

"Want some peanut butter crackers?" called Tattoo.

"No."

His stomach was so tight he couldn't think about eating anything.

"Car coming slow down the alley," said McManaway. "Late-model red Pontiac."

"Real slow," added Clark. "It's passing."

"Could be looking for a parking place," reported Bettles. "No, it's turning down behind me, up to Thomas Street."

A minute later, Caruthers picked it up. "Yeah, it's coming . . . Went on up the hill. Forget it."

Harter didn't know whether to relax because the car had driven on or to tense even more because, still, nothing was happening.

"Coming back down," said Caruthers. "Heading for the Avenue."

"Lights pulling in the alley again," said McManaway. "No, it's backing out on Thomas Street and heading up."

"Same red Pontiac," said Caruthers. "Parking on your side, just below the house."

Harter pulled out his revolver and laid it on the arm of his chair.

It seemed like a year before Caruthers had anything new to add. "Okay, he's getting out. Got a stick—no, a cane—in his hand. Big guy. Looks like light hair. Coming to the door."

"I'm signing off," announced Harter. "You direct, Caruthers."

He had the gun in his right hand and the radio in his left when the knock came. Tattoo was on his feet in an instant but seemed to take forever to open up. The television died. Smart, thought Harter.

"Who is it?" called the old man after moving to the door.

"You wanted to see me," said a voice—a voice Harter recognized. He was right on the money.

The door opened, then closed. He heard the footsteps of the two men but couldn't hear the tap of the cane. Tattoo seemed to return to his overstuffed chair. The other man, he judged, had sat on the daybed.

"Can't say I seen you before," said Tattoo, his voice surprisingly firm. The old man had guts.

"I'm answering your phone call."

"I didn't call you."

"Think of me as a messenger."

"I don't want no messenger."

"You wanted cash, didn't you? I've got it." He heard the cane scrape against the floor, as if the man had moved to take something from his pocket. "I'm the payoff. But, first, you have to earn it. Tell me what you know so I'm sure you're worth it."

There was a long silence. Harter gripped his gun tightly and tried to picture the scene in the front room. He thought he heard Tattoo playing with a tobacco package. He imagined he heard the daybed springs as the big man adjusted his weight.

"What I been told is that Daniel Jones and Simon Bowman come to town sixty years ago with a teenage girl with a wide-open cunt. Named Amelia Logan. I figure she don't want to be reminded of them days no more. I know Bowman was a scab and a thug for old Devendall. Maybe like you. I know him and Daniel died in fires that some blazer set. Maybe that was you, too."

"You old codgers. You pretend these moth-eaten stories are worth something, like the deep dark past always means something."

The voice was cool, not angry, in its contempt. No hot fire crackled through it. Harter guessed the man had been through similar scenes with Jones and Bowman. It was old hat to him. The Amelia Logan stories really had nothing to do with him anyway. But Harter knew how the earlier scenes with Jones and Bowman had turned out. He knew what the cane was for.

"Well, if my story don't mean nothing, why the hell are you here?" Tattoo asked. "Get back in your car and drive away. I'll tell it to someone else. The detective would eat it up."

"Harter?"

"Yeah, that's his name."

"Shit, you know he wouldn't pay you a cent."

"You ain't paid me nothing yet."

Harter heard the daybed springs creak as the man stood up.

"Come closer and I'll slice you up, you son of a bitch!" yelled Tattoo.

Harter was on his feet. Rounding the head of the kitchen steps. Into the living room.

"Drop it, Reverend!"

The cane was held high above the man's red hair, ready to thump the old man in the chair—the old man who held a butcher knife.

For a moment Harter wasn't sure.

For a moment he feared Sam Knotts would follow through and clobber Tattoo.

For a moment he imagined he'd have to blow the preacher to the nearest corner of hell.

Then Knotts lowered his weapon.

"Wise decision, Reverend," said Harter, stepping into the room. "You playing Avenging Angel tonight, or just raising funds for your school?"

Tattoo let out a nervous chuckle, put down his heavy knife, and relaxed into the softness of his chair.

Knotts didn't respond. He faced the floor and squinted at the detective from the corner of his eyes.

Harter raised the radio to call the other cops in. He didn't take his eyes off Knotts for more than an instant, but it was time enough for the cane to lash out and crash against his right wrist. He heard his revolver smash into the television set and saw the picture tube explode glass into the room before he realized he'd lost the gun.

His wrist ached like it was broken. With his left hand, he started to slam the radio into the side of Knotts' head. Too late. The preacher was already bearing down with a fierce blow of the cane to his shoulder, digging into the flesh and glancing off the left side of his neck. Harter crumpled to his knees and dropped the radio.

When he saw Knotts turn toward Tattoo, he scrambled forward, trying to bring the big man down, but he let go of Knotts' legs when the cane rapped his back twice with a vengeance. Collapsing on his belly, he felt a steel-tipped boot grind into his hip.

His brain, overloaded with raw pain, edged toward blurriness.

Where the hell are you, Caruthers!

And then the weight landed on him, and then the quiet.

"You alright?" asked Tattoo, kneeling beside him and lifting his head from the floor. Harter felt the old man's hand rub the slivers of television glass from his face. There was a burning twinge when he moved his head.

"Where is he?"

"I killed him."

Harter twisted his bruised upper body and saw Sam Knotts' football tackle's frame lying across him.

"Pull yourself out from under," said Tattoo.

Only when he was standing could Harter focus on the butcher knife protruding from the red patch between Knotts' shoulder blades. A pissrun of blood ran across the windbreaker toward a puddle of red on the floor.

"Let's go outside," said Harter, wanting out of the room badly.

He stepped around Knotts and, testing his arms and legs, walked slowly to the door. Outside, he waved Caruthers over. The bastard was still in his car. As the other cops showed up and went inside, he lit a cigarette and stayed out in the cool night. He touched his tender wrist. The cane didn't seem to have splintered it.

"I didn't know what to do," said Tattoo.

"You did the right thing," said Harter.

Caruthers came out. "I called headquarters and the coroner. That your killer in there?"

"One of them."

"What now?"

"You mop up. I'm going home." Harter turned to Tattoo.

"Suppose I take you out to the motel to spend the rest of the night with May?"

"I'd like that."

Harter looked at Caruthers. "Tell McManaway to pick me up at my place at nine A.M. in a squad car. Tell him to be in uniform."

··· 30 ···

His body, welted, black and blue, made him sensitive to every bump in the road. He was tired, had only gotten a couple of hours sleep. Mostly he'd laid awake in his apartment, alternating between a yearning for Liz's salving arms and a single-minded drive to be back on the case.

"That's the house," he told Dave McManaway. "Turn in the drive. Park right in front of the door."

There was a side to him that wanted to tell McManaway to put on the siren and make a big show of it for the neighbors, but he didn't.

"You want me to come in with you?" asked McManaway, turning off the engine.

"Yeah, I guess you better."

The maid in the gray-striped uniform answered their knock. "Mr. Devendall has already gone to his office," she said as soon as she recognized Harter.

"I'd like to see Mrs. Devendall," said Harter, stepping stiffly past the maid into the entry hall. "Tell her we know who killed her daughter-in-law."

Without another word, he led McManaway down the hall and into the library. He thought about stationing the young cop on the straight-backed chair outside the door but decided it was best for him to witness everything. Then he sat in the desk chair and waited.

Amy Devendall wasn't long in coming.

"Good morning, Mr. Harter," she said, tossing a sideways glance at McManaway when she entered the room. "Martha says you have news."

She sat on the loveseat, folded her pudgy hands in the lap of her blue dress, and waited for him to say something.

"Your friend Sam Knotts died last night."

"That's awful," she said, her face remaining a rouged blank. "Was it a traffic accident?"

"He was killed while trying to murder an old man. There was a can of kerosene in his car."

"I don't understand."

"He was about to do in a fellow named Henry Kendall, just as he'd done in Daniel Jones and Simon Bowman."

"There are those names again. What do they have to do with Susan?"

"Is the name Amy short for anything, Mrs. Devendall?"

"My name is simply Amy," she said curtly.

Her voice was deceptive in its confidence. Harter sensed she'd grown a shade paler beneath her makeup.

He started again. "Do you like old stories, Mrs. Devendall?"

"Occasionally, if they're short and witty."

"Let me tell you one. It's neither short nor witty, but I think it'll grab you."

"I'm all ears," she said with sarcasm.

"Where to begin?" he mumbled, as if to himself. From the corner of his eye, he watched McManaway watching him. "Once upon a time there was a girl in Wild Stream, West Virginia, by the name of Amelia Logan. Have you ever been to Wild Stream, Mrs. Devendall?"

"I don't recall it, if I have, Detective Harter. Certainly I haven't been through there for a long time, if ever."

"Well, it's a small town. Not much industry. Not much happening. Not very rich. I can understand how a lady of your background might have missed it. You may find parts of this story rather shocking, in fact. If so, I apologize ahead of time. Seems this Amelia Logan found she could generate a certain income with her body. She was a whore. And she was apparently bright. When she learned that two young men—Simon Bowman and Daniel Jones—were taking off for the metropolis of Shawnee, she ran away with them. Bright lights, big city, I suppose."

"When did this happen, Detective?"

"Oh, 1923 or so. I realize you'd have only been a teenage girl yourself. Anyway, soon after the threesome got to Shawnee, Daniel Jones caught on with the railroad and started his own life. Within a couple years he was married and living on Baxter Street in the East End. Simon Bowman wasn't as lucky. He wasn't as hard a worker. He had a mean, wild streak. He worked off and on for the canal until the 1926 flood knocked it out of business for good. After that he sometimes dug ditches. He was scab labor when the railroaders were on strike. For a while he was . . . let's call it a security guard. No, let's be honest. A man named James Howard Devendall hired Simon Bowman to be a thug, a strikebreaker."

"My late husband?" she asked. "Be careful how you throw around names."

"No offense. The names come with the story, that's all. Think of them as fictional characters if you prefer."

"I'd prefer you tell your story and be done with it, Mr. Harter."

"Okay. So James Howard Devendall owns a number of places

along the canal, including a factory building. Simon Bowman probably lives in one of them. Off and on, Amelia Logan is with him. Now Mr. Devendall—I could change the name if it really bothers you, but it does spice things up—Mr. Devendall seems to have been taken by this lovely . . . let's call her a courtesan, not just a whore. Let's say the wealthy old gentleman falls for her hard. Maybe she convinces him she comes from a good Virginia family. Maybe she's got something on him, something she knows Simon Bowman did in his employ. Or, maybe, he really did love her. Old Devendall probably sets her up as his mistress in a classy apartment. Eventually they even marry. There's no license in the courthouse, so they might have gone away for a long honeymoon before returning to introduce the transformed Amelia Logan to west-side society. She's still only in her twenties, very attractive and a fast learner. After a few years, they have a son, so old Devendall has an heir. Meanwhile, Simon Bowman is pretty much a drunk on Shantytown streets. It's easy to shut him up by sending a little bottle money each month or, when he gets older, buying him a trailer outside of town. He just needs to be reminded now and then that the gravy train ends if he ever breathes a word about Amelia Logan or any of the rest of it."

"I'm beginning to get confused, Detective. Surely these things happened almost fifty years ago."

"Yeah, but Simon Bowman lives a long time. The unexpected happens. He gets religion. Stops drinking. A preacher, someone like Sam Knotts, saves him. It's quite an emotional scene. You can probably picture it. There's poor Simon on his knees, pouring out his heart in confession to this Knotts fellow. He wants to be forgiven so badly. Some of the things he wants to be forgiven for might involve James Howard Devendall and Amelia Logan. Could be more than skeletons in the closet. Maybe there were corpses in the canal, a union organizer or two. Well, this preacher, this Sam Knotts, grasps everything quickly. He sees how damaging the tale could be to a fine old family, particularly to someone very concerned about reputation. He calls up Amelia Logan, now a widow, and—let's get down to it—he blackmails her. The man has no more scruples than Amelia Logan does. He's the greedy type, needs money for his empire, wants to build a Christian academy. He soon finds he's met his match in Amelia. She'll pay off, but demands he get rid of Simon Bowman so there's blood on his hands, too. One August night he beats the old man and sets fire to his trailer. For a little reminder to Amelia, he puts up a sign noting his school has received a donation in memory of A.L."

"You probably find all this fascinating, Detective, but I'm starting to be bored by your saga," said Amy Devendall. She turned her body slightly away from him and the movement sent a whiff of her perfume his way.

He looked at McManaway to see if he too was growing bored, but the young cop's eyes were pinned to her.

"I'm almost through, Mrs. Devendall," said Harter. "Seems Amelia Logan worried and worried about Simon Bowman's death. At some point, she realized Daniel Jones was also still around. I'm not sure how she found out. Knotts could have told her. Or maybe her daughter-in-law, a social worker, told her one night over dinner. Perhaps Susan had read Bowman's obituary and mentioned she knew another old man from Wild Stream. It doesn't matter how Amelia Logan found out, does it? What matters is that our righteous preacher paid a visit to Jones two weeks ago and collected another donation."

"I still don't understand," said Amy Devendall. "It's Susan's death I'm concerned about, and your story doesn't seem to have anything to do with her."

"I know. I've been over and over that. It's the oddest-shaped piece, isn't it? But it has the simplest explanation."

"What's that?"

"Chance."

"Chance?"

"Like a man who gets trapped one night between two refrigerator cars coupling. Susan was just in the wrong place at the wrong time."

"You can't be serious, Detective Harter."

"Why not? Shawnee is a small city. I'm sure Amelia Logan has learned it's not nearly as immense as she once thought it was. I'd guess your daughter-in-law was acting out her urge to be photographed and was visiting a photographer on Thomas Street on the night Daniel Jones was murdered. She knew the alley from her social work, so she parked in it. Let's say our friendly preacher was running from Jones' house when she happened along. Knotts didn't know what to do so he forced her into his car and took her with him."

"Do you believe your Amelia Logan would allow her own daughter-in-law to be murdered?"

"Sure, I do. I figure it was a hard decision. Knotts probably kept Susan in his church or house until early Saturday morning when he got the word from Amelia. God knows what happened to her. When Amelia was sure Susan was dead, she called the police and reported her daughter-in-law missing."

"Strange behavior, Detective, for someone as protective of her family name as you believe Amelia Logan was."

"Susan couldn't be trusted to keep family secrets. She was about to run off with a congressman. You know, there was even a temporary side benefit for Amelia and Knotts. The death of Susan threw everyone off. The police and the press were more worried about what happened to her than about what happened to Daniel Jones. No one had noticed Simon Bowman's killing in August."

"Ridiculous. What else can I say? Ridiculous," said Amy Devendall.

Harter couldn't tell if Dave McManaway agreed with her.

"I don't think a smart young prosecutor would have much trouble putting together a case for a grand jury," Harter said. "Any one of the murders is enough to put Amelia Logan away."

"If she's as wealthy as you say, Amelia Logan could hire an equally smart young attorney to shoot your silly story full of holes."

"Yeah, but the press will blow it up nicely. A trial like that would attract reporters from all over, even New York. Shawnee would have its own Lizzy Borden. The Chamber of Commerce would erect a statue to Amelia. She'd love the publicity, I'm sure. No matter what the verdict, she'd live on in legend. The story's got sex and violence, religion and money. If I was Amelia Logan, I'd already be searching for that smart young attorney. Your son won't do. I understand he doesn't take criminal cases. Besides, he could hardly defend the murderer of his wife."

"Are you making an accusation, Detective Harter?" she asked.

"Yeah, I guess I am. Shawnee isn't big enough, is it, Amelia? I was with Henry Kendall when he called you Sunday."

"I received no phone call," she insisted.

"You have the right to remain silent," he told her.

··· 31 ···

Wednesday morning's headlines in *The News* were good enough to sell some papers, thought Harter. He hoped Amy Devendall would see them.

WEST-SIDE WOMAN CHARGED WITH THREE MURDERS.

Beneath it, slightly smaller, was EVANGELIST KILLED DURING ARSON ATTEMPT.

Liz called before he'd even read the articles. She was usually a faster starter in the morning than he was.

"Congratulations, you've solved your case," she said.

"Thanks."

"There's no doubt it was Amy?"

"No," he answered, wondering at her question.

"You promised you'd call me."

"I was going to today."

"Will you be coming over tonight?"

"Yeah. You herd the kids out as early as you can. I'll take you out for dinner."

"Where?"

He wondered how she'd like the diner near the railroad yards. "Have you ever been out to the overlook on the mountain south of town? They used to call it Lover's Leap."

"Are we going to park?" She laughed.

"That's exactly what we're going to do. I haven't made love in a car in years." He rubbed gently at the swollen bruise on his shoulder and hoped it wasn't an insane promise. "Wear something you might have worn to a drive-in twenty years ago."

"I'm not that kind of girl."

"Then you'll find out something new about yourself."

"I'm always finding out something new about myself," she said. "I'll see you tonight."

"Uh . . ."

"What?"

"About the Halloween Party . . ."

"Saturday night?"

"I don't think I can go to the Winhams'."

"Do you have to work?"

"I just don't think I can go."

"We'll talk about it later."

He knew from her voice that, yes, they would talk about it later.

"Bye."

He hung up and lit a cigarette.

He wished she could understand. He'd take her almost anywhere but to the west-side party.

He inhaled and flipped through the newspaper spread in front of him. He stopped when he saw Jack Reese's photo.

The old lady, bent over, picking up a loaf of bread.

The brief caption gave the necessary details and the address of the food bank.

He took another hit of coffee and nicotine.

The train was distant at first but came deeper and deeper into the East End until, for a few minutes, it was louder than the traffic below him.

...

JACK REESE

...

··· 32 ···

I put down *The News* Wednesday morning and stared across the kitchen table at Tattoo.

"You're a hero."

"May called me that, too," he grumbled, rubbing at his stub like he did when he was nervous. "I don't see it that way. Harter set everything up. What'd you expect me to do—let the son of a bitching preacher bloody him up and then turn on me?"

"It was all face-to-face," I explained. "Not like pulling a trigger from a distance or dropping a bomb from the sky. I don't know if I could have done it."

"Sure you could of. Ain't much of a choice between living and dying. I told you the first day—I wanted to get the bastard that murdered Daniel."

"You did, Henry," said May. She rose from the table to refill our coffee cups.

Not only had he rid the world of Sam Knotts but he'd killed the burglar in my dream, as well—that burglar I'd been chasing up and down the dry-as-kindling stories night after night. The nightmare arsonist's visits had gotten briefer since I'd told Harter the truth the Thursday before. After Monday night, he'd completely disappeared.

"He's Bill Harter's son, you know," Tattoo said to May as she sat back down.

"I figured maybe he was."

"Don't know how he ended up a cop."

"Needed a job," I said, remembering the day on the towpath when I'd put the question to him. "He told me he became a detective because he needed a job."

"Shawnee ain't bursting with jobs no more, that's for sure," said Tattoo.

"You don't have to tell me," I said. "That's why I'm a stringer for *The News*, no matter how much you ride me about it. What else can a photographer do around here?"

"They did alright on *this* story," answered Tattoo, with the hint of a smile.

I pushed back from the table and stood up. "I've got to go to work right now."

"Congressman Canley getting his morals certified again?" barked Tattoo.

"I don't think so. I'm going to take pictures at the old passenger station. I've always meant to, and Metling wants one."

"They're not tearing it down, are they?" asked May.

"They keep talking about it."

"You ain't going to recognize this city soon," said Tattoo sadly as I went out the door.

I started to cut through the yard to my old Ford, but changed my mind on the way, deciding I'd walk down the hill to the old Shawnee–Potomac station. I shook away the memory of having once considered posing Susan Devendall à la Marilyn Monroe there.

It was a non-threatening October day and it wasn't far. Growing up, I'd hiked up and down the long hill a million times in all kinds of weather—past Bernhardt's store, now gone, past the Methodist Church, now with its basement food bank, past all the houses, hangouts, lots, and alleys that formed the neighborhood I'd once been secure and comfortable in.

I didn't know if I'd stay long enough in Shawnee to feel security and comfort again.

All I knew for sure was I didn't want to live through the last two weeks again.

I wanted to get ahead of the killings, the arson, the dreams.

If some lady with good legs stepped down onto my porch tomorrow and commissioned a passport photo, I'd ask her some questions.

Might even make her fill out an application.

If she took off her coat and displayed a model's body, I'd pull Harter's card out of my pocket, hand it to her, and announce, "Get my agent's okay."

Then I'd grab my camera and go searching for a photogenic freight.

Hell, if that train stopped, I might even hop a boxcar and see where it went.